What they say about Thomas Trew

'A fascinating fantasy world.' *The School Librarian*

'An extremely captivating and interesting read! It's full of action!' *Elliot, age 9*

'A mind bursting, eye watering adventure! . . . scary and imaginative . . . funny and fantastic.' *Cerian, age 10*

'I couldn't put it down. The best book I've ever read . . . and I mean it!' *Kyle, age 9*

'Fabulous, mind capturing.' *Jay, age 9½*

'I would give this book six shiny stars out of five!' *Sarah, age 10*

'It's a very addicting story and thrilling twists that makes you want to read on and on.' *Matthew, age 12*

'. . . six rumbustious adventures, it enjoys Blytonesque jollities and gorgeous grotesques drawn b   *Times*

THOMAS TREW
AND THE ISLAND OF GHOSTS

SOPHIE MASSON

Illustrated by Ted Dewan

Hodder
Children's
Books

A division of Hachette Children's Books

For Zoë Barker-Smith

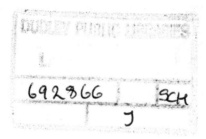

Dear Reader,

Do you wish you could leave the ordinary world and go into an extraordinary one, full of fun and magic and adventure – and danger? You do? Well, so does Thomas Trew and one grey London afternoon, his wish comes true!

Two amazing people come calling – a dwarf called Adverse Camber and a bright little lady named Angelica Eyebright. They tell Thomas he's a Rymer and that he has a destiny in their world, the world of the Hidden People. Rymers link the Hidden World and the world of humans, which is known as the Obvious World, and they can travel easily between them. And so Angelica and Adverse ask him to come and live in their village, Owlchurch, deep in the Hidden World.

It's a world of magic – what the Hidden People call 'pishogue'. It's a world of extraordinary places and people – the Ariels, who live in the sky; the Seafolk, who live in the ocean; the Montaynards, who live in the rocks and mountains; the Uncouthers, who live deep underground; and the Middlers, who live on the surface of the Earth. Not everyone in the Hidden World is pleasant or friendly, and some of them, like the Uncouthers, are very nasty indeed.

All kinds of adventures are waiting for Thomas in the Hidden World. And this is just one of them. Look out for the others, too!

ONE

Patch saw it first. It was early morning
and she was out gathering herbs with
her mother, Old Gal, near the steep
river bank. Patch had just scrambled down to
pick some flowers, when she had a sudden
strange feeling. The kind that makes your hair
stand on end and your palms prickle and your
skin creep.

She looked up. There was something rising
out of the river. At first, she couldn't make out
what it was, because it was covered in smoky,
grey mist. It was big, and getting bigger. She
couldn't move or cry out as slowly the mist
began to clear.

And there was an island. Smooth, glassy

black rock, where patches of mist and smoke still clung like cobwebs. On the side facing Patch was what looked like a door, set into the rock. It was large, and glowed red and gold. Apart from this, there was absolutely nothing on the island. Nothing stirred or moved. Yet somehow Patch felt more

frightened than she had ever been in her whole life. She wanted to run away. She wanted to scream. She wanted to call her mother. But she couldn't do anything.

The door opened. Mist swirled out and the outline of a man appeared. Then the mist blew away and Patch could see him clearly. He was

tall but hunchbacked, with a long, thin, black moustache flowing to his waist, black eyes, and long, hair in a pigtail. He wore a shining, black robe, and a black cap, and carried a staff in one hand.

He looked straight at Patch and lifted his staff. Suddenly, she heard a voice in her head, saying, over and over, 'Danger – Rymer – danger – Rymer – danger – Rymer . . .' Patch tried to speak, to ask questions, but she couldn't. Then the words faded away. The mist gathered, and very soon both man and door vanished from sight. But the island itself did not disappear, looming black beyond the mist.

Suddenly Patch found her legs and her voice. Yelling, tripping over herself, she scrambled up the river bank. 'Mother! There's a black island! A man! Thomas – he's in danger! Mother, come and see! Come and see!'

Old Gal went with her down to the river. She stared silently at the mist-shrouded island. She was silent so long that Patch couldn't stand it. She shouted, 'Mother! Oh, what is it? It's bad, isn't it? Oh, tell me!'

'It's the Island of Ghosts,' said Old Gal, quietly.

'What's that? What's it doing here?' asked Patch, shuddering. Most people in the Hidden World don't have anything to do with ghosts if they can help it. The world of ghosts is different both to the Hidden World and the human or Obvious World. Sometimes ghosts will get stuck between worlds, or haunt the Obvious World. But they hardly ever go near the Hidden World.

'Don't be afraid. There are only Rymer ghosts on the island,' said Old Gal, gently. 'And it appears in the Riddle only if a living Rymer is in mortal danger, in our world. It appears so we can warn and protect them.'

'Then it's true! Thomas is in danger!'

'Yes. But wait a moment. Tell me exactly what this man looked like. And what he said.'

Patch described him. 'And he just kept repeating: danger – Rymer.'

'I see,' said Old Gal. She was frowning. 'You've described the Guardian, who looks after the island and its people. But why is this happening now? Thomas is sick, but he is getting better. He even sat up and ate something yesterday. It doesn't make sense. Why didn't the island appear before, when he was really very ill?'

'I want to go and warn Thomas, right now!' said Patch, beginning to run.

'No,' said her mother, sharply. 'He's still very weak. The shock could make him relapse. We're going to have a meeting of everyone in Owlchurch and Aspire, and decide what to do and how we can protect him.'

'Me and Pinch too?'

'No, you and your brother are to stay out of it,' said Old Gal, firmly. 'It's too dangerous for children.'

'But I saw it first! And the Guardian spoke to *me*!' cried Patch.

'It doesn't matter,' said her mother. 'You

have no idea how to deal with the Ghost World. If you meddle, you might put Thomas as well as yourselves in very great danger. Neither you nor Pinch are to say anything to Thomas, until we can work out what to do. Do you promise?' She looked fiercely at her daughter, who nodded, reluctantly.

'Promise.'

'Good. Now let's go. No. Don't forget the basket. We still need to make ointments, you know, island or no island.' She turned and was off, briskly, without turning her head.

Patch trudged glumly after her mother, but at the top of the bank, she turned and looked back. The island still sat in the middle of the River Riddle, its glassy, black shape cutting through the greyness around it. I don't like it, thought Patch, shivering. I don't like it at all. I'm sure Thomas will be in much more danger if he doesn't know about this . . . I wish I hadn't promised Mother. I really wish I hadn't . . . I've got to talk to Pinch. It's not fair. Why shouldn't we help? We've got magic powers too. And Thomas is our best friend. And we're not scared of silly old ghosts!

Well, maybe the last bit wasn't really true. But after all, together, she and Pinch and Thomas had gone through all kinds of adventures and braved many dangers, so just how much more dangerous could this one be?

She was about to find out just that.

TWO

Thomas lay in bed. His eyes were closed, but he wasn't asleep. He heard the door of his room open, and his father's voice, and then Angelica Eyebright's. He didn't open his eyes. He knew what they were doing – checking on him again. But though he felt better than before, he was still weak. His head felt like it was wrapped in fog.

Thomas had been sick in bed ever since he was brought home to Owlchurch, half dead, from the terrible adventure of the Flying Huntsman in the land of the Ariels. That was the worst ordeal he had faced in all his time in the Hidden World. Unlike most human beings, he was a Rymer, and welcome in the Hidden World. But not everyone was friendly. Some were very dangerous enemies indeed, including those you didn't expect.

Thomas was glad to be safe in Owlchurch, but it was tiresome being ill. Yesterday, when he'd sat up in bed for the first time, his friends Pinch and Patch Gull were there to greet him. It was good to see them. But after only a few minutes, he became tired again and had to lie down.

He spent a lot of time sleeping. And he had long dreams. Most were healing dreams specially made for him by Morph Onery, the famous Dream-maker of Owlchurch. Some were dreams that came straight out of the magic dream-bed on which he lay. And once or twice, Dr Fantasos, the Dream-maker of Aspire, across the river, had whipped up a flash dream for him. But this morning, he had a different kind of dream.

In it, he was in a funfair, on a kind of giant

merry-go-round. It had carriages shaped like large acorn cups, dangling down on thin silver wires. Thomas sat in one of the carriages. Music started, the merry-go-round creaked into life, and it began to go round. Faster and faster it went, and the wires holding the carriages shook and shivered, the carriage whirred madly. Faster, faster went the merry-go-round, and then suddenly Thomas could feel the wires of his carriage breaking, one by one – *snap, snap, snap!* Then the carriage came off and flew through the air, and he saw, beneath him, long, thin, grey fingers of fog, groping for him . . .

He woke up then and found his father bending over him, an anxious look on his face. 'What's up, Thomas? You sounded scared. Or in pain.'

'No – I'm OK,' Thomas stammered. 'A dream. Just a dream, Dad.'

'That Morph,' said his father, crossly. 'Surely he wouldn't have made you a frightening dream. I've got a good mind to—'

'Of course Morph wouldn't make anything frightening,' said Adverse Camber, the dwarf, beside him. 'You know we don't deal in nightmares.'

'Uncouthers do,' said Gareth. 'Maybe they've managed to send it to Thomas.'

'It wasn't exactly frightening,' said Thomas, frowning a little, trying to remember it properly, for it was fading fast from his mind. 'It made me feel a bit weird, though. I think I was in a kind of funfair . . .'

Adverse Camber shrugged. 'Then it was just a wild dream,' he said. 'A left-over thing, bits and pieces cobbled together. Nothing wrong with that. It does happen sometimes.'

'Mmm,' said Thomas, drowsily and, closing his eyes again, went into a dreamless sleep.

But now, he was fully awake again. He could hear their voices, murmuring. Suddenly, there was a commotion and he heard Old Gal's voice, very sharp. 'I tell you, there's little time to lose and, with Thomas as he is, we don't have the choice to—'

She was cut off by Angelica. 'Shh! Thomas is asleep. Let's go and talk outside.'

'I'm awake,' whispered Thomas, opening his eyes – but too late, as the door slammed. He was alone again.

What was wrong? It had sounded urgent. And something he should help with. After all, he was a Rymer. But what could he do, weak like this? He tried to will himself to sit up. He couldn't do it straight away, so he rolled cautiously on to his side, pushed himself on to one elbow, then tried to sit up that way. Ow! Ow! His limbs ached, and he had a very painful crick in the neck. But by gritting his teeth, he was finally able to lever himself up. Now just to take a few deep breaths, and he might try to swing his legs out of bed and get up.

After a little while, he managed to get to the edge of the bed. He put his legs slowly down.

His head swam and his legs felt weak. But he managed, very carefully, to put his feet on the floor. He thought, I can't just walk by myself, and looked around for something he could lean on. His eyes lighted on a smart, carved walking stick by the bedside table. It had obviously been forgotten by someone who'd come in to see him. In fact it looked like something Dr Fantasos might use. Thomas leaned carefully towards it. His head swam again, but he managed to hook the walking stick. He grasped it hard and, leaning heavily on it, slowly got to his feet.

His legs wobbled and trembled, like jelly. He fell back on the bed. I'm not going to be defeated, he thought, and felt, with each second, as if strength was returning to him. *I have to get up*. He tried again, and this time stood a little longer before he fell back again. Once more he tried, and this time he stayed standing. *Now to walk*, he thought. Very carefully, he took a step away from the bed.

His legs trembled, but he didn't fall down. He took another step. And another. And another. He had to stop then and take a breath. He took another step and came closer to the window. Closer still, and now he could see out of the window, into the street below.

Everyone's down there! he thought. That was just how it looked, as if the whole of Owlchurch was out there, milling around, talking. And look, there come Lady Pandora and Mr Tamblin, Thomas thought, as he saw the big, white car of the mayors of Aspire come sailing down the road that led to Owlchurch. What on earth is going on? I have to find out . . . Hang on. Where are Pinch and Patch? He looked past the crowd to the river. The Gull twins were often to be found there. But he couldn't see them. They must be home. Did they know about what was happening? They must, because the Gull twins always sniffed out things. But now he was getting tired. His head felt strange. He had to get back to bed. He would ask Pinch and Patch when they came up to see him.

But the exercise had tired him a good deal. He was no sooner back in his bed than he really fell asleep. And so when Pinch and Patch looked in on him a little while later, he was deeply asleep and not to be woken.

THREE

'I know what we've got to do to help Thomas,' said Patch, as they slowly went back down the stairs. 'In fact, there's only one thing we can do, really.'

'Really? What's that?' Pinch said, vaguely.

'We've got to go to the Island of Ghosts ourselves and find out what they know,' said Patch, in a rush.

Pinch groaned. 'I was afraid you'd say that. That's what I thought too.'

Brother and sister looked at each other. 'Rymer ghosts are bound to be more friendly than other sorts of spooks,' said Patch, hesitantly.

'Bound to,' said Pinch, glumly.

'Why would they want to hurt us?' said Patch.

'What *could* they do to hurt us?' said Pinch.

'We need to find out,' said Patch. 'I know there's a book on the Ghost World in Monotype Eberhardt's bookshop.'

'Yes, but if we ask to see it, he'll know what we're doing,' said Pinch. 'And he'll tell Mother. And you know we'll be grounded for years if she finds out we're disobeying her. We're too young even to think of meddling with the Ghost World, she'll say.'

'Nonsense,' said Patch, briskly. 'How can we learn to deal with it if we don't get any practice?' She looked hard at Pinch. 'Are you scared, Pinch?'

'Course not,' said Pinch, a little too loudly. 'But I'm just telling you that's what people will say.'

'Who cares?' said Patch, defiantly. 'Do you want to help me or not?'

'Did I say I wouldn't?' snapped Pinch.

'OK, then, first thing is getting into the bookshop and finding the book, right? That'll be easy. Everyone's busy talking out there, Monotype included. I'll get into the bookshop by the back way, you can keep watch at the front.'

'Hey,' said Pinch, indignantly, 'how come I get the boring job?' But Patch didn't answer. She was already on her way.

As Patch had thought, it was easy getting into the bookshop. Monotype was busy talking with the others out in the street, and he'd even left the back door propped open. She crept into the small, cosy shop, and headed straight for the stairs to the mezzanine, where the wilder books were kept in reinforced glass cabinets. Books in the Hidden World don't behave quietly like books in the Obvious World. They have minds of their own, like animals, and like animals, there are all sorts, from the calm and gentle to the fierce and dangerous. Patch had been in the bookshop often enough to know that some of the books might take it into their pages to flap loudly at the sight of an intruder, so she had 'thinned' herself (as the Hidden People call making yourself invisible). The more sensitive books might be able to smell her, but she hoped they wouldn't make too much of a fuss. She knew a soothing little rhyme for them anyway, which went:

Dearest book,
I'm no crook,
but a friend,
to the end.

She'd heard Monotype say it a few times to the more skittish books and it always worked. It did now. The shop stayed fairly quiet, with only a few anxious rustlings, as she made her way to the mezzanine floor. Outside, she could see Pinch hanging around, trying to make himself look inconspicuous. It was no use thinning near the crowd of people; they'd know, and it would make them suspicious.

Patch looked into the cabinets. The books in there really didn't look very pleasant. Many of them had once belonged to evil sorcerers and poisoners; the most notorious was the book of curses called Maldict, which had been a big part of an earlier adventure*.

To Patch's relief, Maldict was now safely locked away on its own. She scanned the titles. *Midnight Magic of Malevolent Might. Ghastly Spells to Flummox Your Enemies. A Sorcerer's Guide on How to Destroy the World in Ten Easy Lessons.* And other such things. No use to her.

Ah! On this next shelf, here were books of travel and geography into strange and dangerous places. *The Wilder Shores of the Hidden World. How to Get on With Uncouthers. Journey Into a Syren's World. Dangerous People in the Obvious World and How to Spot Them. Creatures of Mirkengrim.*

* *Thomas Trew and the Selkie's Curse*

Then she saw it, the exact right thing. It was called *An Atlas of Fantomundi, also known as Ghost World, Complete with Exhaustive Guide to Its Inhabitants, Their Manners, and Customs, by a Wily Wizard of Maximum Repute.* With its plain, grey cover and long, dull title, it did not look like a dangerous book, only very old, shabby and rather down-at-heel. But as Patch stared at it, bright red words appeared on the cover of the book. *My maker died to bring you this book*, it said. *Beware.*

'Nonsense,' said Patch, loudly. 'You're only saying that to frighten me. You were written by a wizard. An Obbo. I'm a Hidden Worlder. I don't die as easily as a human, wizard or not wizard.' Still, her hands trembled as she reached up to the nail where she knew Monotype kept the key of this cabinet, and carefully unlocked the door, saying her little rhyme several times, very fast, so the books might be confused by the buzzing. She reached up to the ghost book, and pulled at it.

It came down easily and crashed on to the floor, making the other books shove and push and growl. Quickly, she slammed the door and locked it again. She looked at the book at her feet. It hadn't moved but lay there limply, like a dead fish. She bent down gingerly to touch it. Still it didn't move. But when she picked it up, it gave a kind of sigh, then flopped open in Patch's hands.

The Island of Ghosts, she read on the top of the page. There was a drawing, of the island she'd seen rising from the river. But the rest of it was blank. 'Well, you're a clever book,' she said, rather warily. 'You knew just what I wanted. But I need information more than a picture.'

The book sighed again. Words suddenly appeared on the page,

under the drawing. *Child, you have been warned. You still wish to proceed?*

'Of course I do,' said Patch, a little crossly. 'Or I wouldn't have got you down, would I?'

The earlier words disappeared. Others appeared. *You ask questions*, ran the words on the page now. *I answer, if I can. It takes time.*

'I don't have time,' said Patch. 'Someone might come.'

Take me out with you, said the book.

'Wait a moment,' said Patch, suspiciously. 'You might run away, if I take you out of here.'

Where would I go? said the book. *I am a book. I belong on a shelf, not in the wild.*

'But Monotype will know you're gone . . .'

The keeper of books does not always look every day, said the book, and the words ran eagerly now. *You take me out, ask me questions. When you have what you want, you can put me back. No one will know.*

'You seem very keen to go out,' said Patch, sternly. 'Why?'

The book sighed, deeply. Words that ran

like tears appeared. *My maker was a great wizard who spent much time in his study. But he also loved the sun and the trees. For his sake I should like to see them. That is all.*

'I see,' said Patch, rather touched. 'Oh well, I suppose you'll be all right. You seem quiet enough.'

Oh I am, said the book.

'Why did Monotype put you in the Dangerous Books section, then?'

My subject. It makes people uneasy. But I am quiet. And very helpful too. You'll need me, to help your friend.

'You know about that?' said Patch, startled.

It is my business to know, said the book. *The study of Fantomundi is the study of the world after Mister D has done his work, and your friend has been close to Death's list. Still is . . .*

'Oh dear,' said Patch. 'That's what I was afraid of. There's a warning that—'

We have little time, said the book, and the words looked spiky and cross. *I will not answer here. Take me out, quickly. Ask me then all you need.*

'My brother will also want to ask,' said Patch.

Yes, yes, said the book. *No more talk. Time to go, child.*

'They'll see you . . .' began Patch, a little annoyed by the bossiness of the book.

No, no, said the book. *Put me in your pocket.* And so saying, it twisted, and shrank, and shrank, till it was about the size of a postage stamp. Gingerly, she put it in her pocket. It gave a tiny sigh, and settled there quietly.

I hope I've done the right thing, thought Patch, as she scrambled back down the stairs and out of the back of the shop – just in time, as in the next second, Monotype came in through the front door and stood for an instant, puzzled. Was something wrong? Then he shook his head, smiled, and went back to work. He must have been imagining things.

FOUR

Thomas woke a few hours later to find Old Gal bending over him, taking his pulse. He smiled weakly at her. 'Hello,' he whispered.

'Don't bother talking, Thomas. You'll only get tired.' Old Gal dropped his hand and rummaged in the bag she was carrying, pulling out some little bottles. 'Now, I've got some mixtures I want you to take.'

'I've already taken some medicine—' Thomas began.

Old Gal broke in. 'These are different. They're super-strength mixtures and will make you strong enough so we can take—' She broke off, suddenly. 'Well, never mind.'

'But—' Thomas began.

She put a finger to her lips. 'Quiet, please. These need quiet to work.' And putting one thin hand under his head, she helped him sit up. With the other hand, she gently put the first bottle to his lips. It was filled with a bright golden liquid.

'What is it?' Thomas tried to say, but the liquid was already in his mouth. It tasted sweet, like honey, and smelled like perfume. Old Gal put the bottle down and took up another, which was full of a dark green liquid. She tipped the bottle to his lips. This time the mixture tasted and smelled horrible, like fermented grass mixed with tar. Thomas spluttered.

'Now, now,' said Old Gal, briskly wiping up the mess. 'Just one more, Thomas.'

'No,' said Thomas, turning his head. 'I don't want—'

'Sorry, son, but you have to,' said his father, coming in at that moment.

He looked rather pale, thought Thomas.

'You want to get well, don't you?' went on Gareth, trying to smile. 'You don't want to lie here for ever?'

'I've already walk—' began Thomas, but again the mixture – a bright red mixture that tasted like a sharp-but-nice apple – went down his throat and he never finished his sentence.

Gareth sat on the bed beside him. 'We'll soon have you up and ready to travel,' he said.

Thomas stared at him. 'Where?'

'Back home.'

'What do you mean? We *are* home!'

'Back to London.'

London? Thomas stared at his father in dismay. They'd left London months and months ago. In fact, it felt like years ago. He had thought they would never go back, that they would always stay in the Hidden World. 'But I don't want to!'

'You *have* to go back,' said Angelica, coming in. Her voice was gentle. 'Even a Rymer can't always live in the Hidden World. And you have been so ill, Thomas. We could not send you back straight away, because you would have died on the way. But now you are a little better and, with Old Gal's mixtures inside of you, you will be fit enough to travel. We leave this very hour.'

'No, no,' cried Thomas, distraught. 'I don't want to go! I want to stay . . . There's still so much I can learn . . . so much for me to do . . . you can't just send me away. I'll be careful, I promise. I won't get into any more adventures . . . Please . . . I can't go. I'll miss everyone so much, especially Pinch and Patch . . .'

'I'm sorry, Thomas,' said Old Gal, gently. 'But it is the only thing to do, in the circumstances.'

'But why now? Why now? Please – give me time to get used to the idea. A few more days . . .weeks. Please!'

'We can't,' said Angelica, softly. 'There are . . . well . . . there are good reasons why not. I'm sorry, Thomas, but that's how it is. You must get back to your own world. Oh, you can come back to us, later – when you're older and stronger.'

'No,' said Thomas, fiercely. 'No. I won't go.'

'Dearest Thomas,' said his father, taking one of his hands, 'please, don't be upset. It's for the best. And London's not so bad, is it? We'll be together, and Lily Lafay – well, she's living just a few doors down from our old house, and we can . . .' He trailed off as Thomas gave him a withering look.

'I don't care about Lily! You love her, but I don't!'

Gareth sighed. 'You just need time to get to know her properly, Thomas, and—'

'No! I don't want to! And she needn't think she can take Mum's place!' Thomas' mother had died many years ago, but sometimes, as now, he still missed her, terribly. The image of her, with her long hair and her gentle face and her flute, had helped to save him, in his first adventure, in the darkness of

Uncouther country and in the last terrible ordeal in Ariel country*. 'She needn't think that!' he repeated, fiercely.

'She doesn't,' said Gareth, helplessly. 'Thomas, please . . . I'm sure people can come and visit us, Angelica, and Adverse, and Pinch and Patch . . .'

'I'm sure we can,' said Angelica, heartily.

Thomas stared at her, then at Old Gal and his father. Anger stirred in him, but he said, quietly, 'Do Pinch and Patch know I have to go?'

Angelica looked quickly at Old Gal, and answered, 'Er . . . not yet.'

'I don't want to leave without saying goodbye to them.'

'Of course you don't,' said Angelica, even more heartily. 'Where are they, Old Gal?'

'Messing around as usual, I suppose,' said the twins' mother, absently.

*A tale told in *Thomas Trew and the Hidden People*.

'I want them to come up and see me now,' said Thomas. He glared at the adults. 'I want to see them alone.' He didn't miss the adults' quick glance at each other. 'Alone,' he repeated, stubbornly. 'Then I promise I'll go without a fuss.'

'Thomas,' said Angelica, very seriously, 'you'd better not think of changing things. You really do have to go. It's a matter of life and death, my dear.'

A little shiver crept over Thomas, but he held Angelica's gaze steadily. 'I promise I'll go without a fuss,' he repeated.

'Very well,' said Angelica. 'You can see Pinch and Patch alone.'

'But if they suggest anything silly,' said Old Gal, 'you must refuse. Do you understand?'

Thomas nodded. 'Won't you tell me why you really want me to go so quickly?' he asked.

If they'd answered him truthfully then, maybe things would have been different. But the three adults looked at each other, then

Angelica said, slowly, 'We've told you. You just need to be back in the Obvious World, and right away.'

'OK,' said Thomas, and closed his eyes, not wanting to talk any more. He knew for sure now they weren't telling the truth. Something was obviously very wrong. Well! If they wouldn't trust him, neither would he trust them.

He heard them murmuring to each other, then they left the room. There was silence for a few minutes, quickly broken by the sound of footsteps tearing up the stairs and, a few seconds later, the Gull twins burst into the room.

'Thomas! Thomas! Are you OK? They said you have to leave!' Patch was beside herself. There were bright red spots on her greenish cheeks, and her eyes were shining with angry tears. 'It's not true, is it, Thomas? Is it?'

'Yes,' said Thomas, 'it is,' and embarassed himself terribly – and Pinch too – by suddenly bursting into tears. 'Sorry,' he snuffled, 'I'm stupid, I didn't mean to . . .' And then he howled again. 'I hate London! I don't want to go back there! I want to stay here!'

'We want you to stay here too,' said Pinch. 'We do, we really do.'

'I don't understand why I've got to go now,' said Thomas, scrubbing angrily at his eyes, 'It's not fair, I'm getting better and so it should be better for me now!'

Pinch and Patch looked at each other. Thomas saw it. 'How come everyone knows something I don't!' he shouted. 'What's happened? Why is everyone suddenly so keen for me to go back? Come on, tell me. Am I your friend or aren't I?'

'Of course you're our friend,' said Patch, half crying herself, 'but we promised not to say, and . . .'

'Is it something about the Hidden World or something about me?' said Thomas.

Pinch and Patch nodded, miserably. 'Both,' said Pinch.

'Well, then, I've got a right to know!'

Patch looked at her brother and nodded. He put a finger to his lips and leaned towards Thomas. 'You've got to be quiet if we tell you. The Island of Ghosts – it's appeared in the Riddle.'

Thomas stared. 'What's that?'

In a rush Patch said, 'Well, it's part of Fantomundi – Ghost World – it's where the ghosts of Rymers hang out. And it only appears here when a Rymer is in mortal danger. That's why they want you to go back.'

Thomas said, 'But if I'm in mortal danger, wouldn't I be just as much in the Obvious World?'

'I don't know,' said Patch, unhappily. 'But I think I heard them say that you were in danger in *this* world.'

'But in danger from what?'

'Nobody knows. At least, nobody here.'

'But the ghost people – they'd know, wouldn't they? Because they warned about it?'

'I suppose so,' said Patch, shooting a quick look at her brother.

'If that's where Rymers go when they die,' said Thomas, dreamily, 'Mum would be there, wouldn't she? She'd tell me. She'd help me fight whatever it was . . . I could go over to that island and speak to her . . .'

'No, no,' said Patch. 'It's not safe. Ghosts – you never know what they might do, and—'

'Don't be silly,' said Thomas, angrily. 'This is my mother we're talking about. She loved me! She wouldn't hurt me.'

'No,' said Pinch, 'but . . .'

'But what? Oh, I see. *You're* the ones scared of ghosts!'

'We are not!' said Pinch, indignantly. 'In fact, we were going to try and get in there ourselves, and find out what was the prob—'

'Pinch!' cut in his sister, but too late. Thomas had heard enough.

'So you were going to go there, were you?' he said, sharply. 'You were going to find out for yourselves, and not even tell me! Well, I'm coming with you! I don't want to run away to the Obvious World, I want to find out what's really wrong, and I want to fight it! I'm not scared!'

'But Thomas, you're ill . . .' said Patch, helplessly, as Thomas flung back the sheets with a strength he hadn't felt in many days. He swung his legs off the bed, and was even able to get up without the aid of the cane. Maybe it was Old Gal's medicine or just the power of his anger and determination, but he suddenly felt able to face anything.

'Come on, then, what do we do first?'

'But Thomas . . .' began Patch.

Pinch jabbed her in the side with a sharp elbow. 'Stop it, Patch. You can see he wants to do it. And it is about him, anyway. OK. We'll have to thin to get out of here and down to the river unseen, Thomas. Do you think you can cope with that?'

Thomas nodded.

'OK, take each other's hands,' said Pinch, 'and let's say the words. Patch, you've still got that silly book in your pocket, haven't you?'

'Don't talk like that about it,' whispered Patch, patting her pocket, 'it'll feel offended and won't help us. Just a book about Fantomundi we found in Monotype's bookshop,' she explained, seeing Thomas's bewildered look. 'It's a complete guide and will help us get there and back safely.'

'You stole it?' said Thomas, eyes round.

'No, I just took it for a walk,' said Patch, frostily. 'It wanted to go. It wanted to help us.'

'I bet,' said Pinch, in an undertone, winking at Thomas, who suddenly felt very much better.

'Well, at least we've got something to start with. Let's do it!'

FIVE

The island was still there, half muffled in its trailing scarf of mist. 'I don't like the look of it much,' said Pinch. 'Neither do I,' said Patch, in a small voice.

But Thomas shrugged. He really didn't feel scared at all, only excited. 'Why should you be scared? Rymers are friends of the Hidden World. Now, how do we get over there?'

Patch took the book out of her pocket. As she did so, it grew in her hand so that when she opened it and turned to the page on the Island of Ghosts, it was normal size again. She said, 'Dear book, we need to get into the island. How do we do it?'

Immediately, red words appeared on the

page. *Danger,* they said, *danger. Can I persuade you not to go?*

'No,' said Thomas, 'we must go. At least, I must. I want to talk to my mother. I'm a Rymer, and she was a Rymer too. I need her help.'

Good day to you, Rymer, said the book, promptly. *It is a most fine day, is it not?*

'Yes, yes,' said Thomas, impatiently, 'but please tell us – how do we get in there?'

Not a good idea for you to go, said the book, in firm black letters. *Ghost World is not the same as the Hidden World. Very dangerous. Hidden Worlders can fade away to nothing there, vanish like a puff of smoke. Ghost World is hard on humans too; you can get trapped and die there, easily. My maker did . . .*

'Well, I won't,' said Thomas, stoutly. 'I won't, because my mother will protect me. She has a special magic. She protected me in the Uncouthers' land. I would have died if she hadn't saved me in Ariel country—'

That's as may be, said the book, in spiky

letters. *But it will still be dangerous.*

'I'm prepared for that,' said Thomas.

In any case, you should go alone. The Hidden Worlders should not go. It is very unsafe for them to be too close to ghosts too long.

'Then they will stay here,' said Thomas. 'I'll go on my own.'

'How dare you! We'll decide what we do,' said Patch, fiercely. She turned back to the book. 'He's our friend, and he's been very sick. We can help him. We'll go too.'

You are a silly child, said the book in sharp, bright letters. *If you stay more than a short time there, you will fade away and vanish. It is worse than for humans, who may meet Mister D but still be around as ghosts.*

'Who's Mister D?' said Thomas.

Pinch and Patch looked quickly at each other. 'He's . . . he's . . . the one in charge of death. When your name comes up in his files, he comes to fetch you.'

Thomas couldn't help a shiver.

You may well shiver, said the book, in big, important letters. *Meeting Mister D is no joke. But it's even worse for Hidden Worlders in the world of ghosts. If they overstay, they simply cease to exist, completely, in any way. Do you understand?*

'You said a short time,' said Patch, swallowing. 'How short is short?'

For the time it takes for a bracelet of grass to wither, said the book, in big, black letters.

'What does that mean?'

You make a bracelet of grass out of grass stems from your world, said the book. *You tie them around your wrist. While they are still green, you are safe. Once they start to wither, you are in trouble. Once they have withered completely, it's too late for you, human or Hidden-Worlder.*

'That's quite a while,' said Pinch, airily.

Not as long as you might think. Time passes differently in the Ghost World, said the book.

'More quickly or slower?'

It depends, said the book.

'Then if we do what you say – make those

bracelet things – we are OK till they start withering?'

That's what I told you, isn't it? said the book, huffily.

'You have heard of people doing this?'

Yes. Only once or twice, mind.

'And those people came back to the Hidden World, safe and sound?' said Patch.

Well, safe, said the book. *Sound, not so sure. I heard they carried the air of the Ghost World with them and were never the same again. They did not live as long as other Hidden Worlders.*

'You can't do this,' said Thomas, to his friends. 'I really, really appreciate it, but it's too dangerous . . .'

'Oh, stop it,' said Patch, crossly. 'It's dangerous for you too, if you meet Mister D. But we'll make sure you won't.' To the book, she said, 'Is it true that when the Island of Ghosts appears, it's only because the Rymer is in mortal danger?'

Oh yes, said the book, in sharp, dark letters.

That is certain. The Rymer is in mortal danger. The island would never have appeared otherwise, or the Guardian spoken his warning.

'Then this Guardian – or other people on the island – they could tell him why, and what threatens him?'

It's possible, snapped the book.

'Very well, then. Tell us how to get there, and stop wasting time.'

It would be irresponsible of me to tell you any more than I've already said. I must say that— began the book, in indignant red letters, when Pinch snatched it out of his sister's hands.

'Look, my friend,' he said, threateningly, 'if you don't tell us what we want to know, straight away, I'm going to rip you into little pieces and throw you into the river. Or turn you into a frog, or glamour up a huge silverfish that will eat you alive.'

The book gave a jerk, trying to pull out of his hands. Jagged words appeared on its pages. *How dare you speak to me like this! You are a wicked boy. You will come to a bad end.*

'You'll come to it quicker than me,' said Pinch, and he took hold of one of the pages. 'Now, come on, book – what's it to be?'

You are a fool, said the book. *You are all fools. Very well. Do as you wish! Don't say I didn't warn you. I will tell you this, and this only. Put on your grass bracelets, and call on the Guardian. He will tell you what to do.*

'Is that all? There's no password?' asked Thomas.

But the page stayed blank. Pinch said, 'Come on, book, tell us more, or I'll . . .' But as he spoke, the book gave a mighty jerk, tore itself out of his hands, leaped on to the ground, and before anyone could stop it, had scuttled to a nearby hole in the river bank, disappearing down it faster than it takes time to say it.

'You idiot, Pinch!' cried Patch. 'Now we don't have a guide!'

'Who cares?' said Pinch. 'Useless smug thing. It didn't really know anything worth knowing. Good riddance.'

She wailed, 'But it's gone now! Monotype's going to be so angry!'

Thomas said, 'Never mind that now. Let's make those bracelets.'

Quickly, they picked some long grass stems, plaited them together and made three bracelets, which they slipped over their wrists. Then they walked close to the river's edge. Thomas said, softly, 'Guardian of the Island of Ghosts, I am the Rymer, and these are my friends. We wish to speak with you.'

Where the words had come from, he couldn't say. But they died away, suddenly the mist around the island began to lift, and a glowing gold-and-red door appeared. Slowly, it opened, and the old man came out. He looked straight at Thomas, and raised his staff.

'Rymer and son of a Rymer,' he said, and this time his voice rang out clearly across the water. 'What is it you wish to ask? If you wish to know what exactly threatens you, I cannot tell you, for I am forbidden to do so. I can only warn of danger.'

'But my mother, who was also a Rymer, is on the island. She loves me. Even if she does not know, she may be able to help me find out. Will you let us come? Will you open the door for us?'

The Guardian's eyes flickered. He said, 'The living are as shadows on the island, while the ghosts are the more solid. This will not be easy for you. And it may be easier to come here than to return.'

'I still want to do it,' said Thomas. 'I don't want to run away to London. I want to know why I'm in danger, and what from.'

'You won't have much time to find out,' said the Guardian. 'I warn you.'

'Please, let me take the chance!' cried Thomas.

'Very well, because you are an important Rymer – and a brave one – you will be allowed to enter, for a short time. And one of your friends may come too. But only one. The other must stay and keep watch and help you return.'

'I'll come,' said Patch.

'No, I will,' said Pinch.

'Please, don't argue,' said Thomas, hurriedly. He picked up a pebble from the path and put his hands behind his back, shifting the stone. 'Let's do it this way. Whoever guesses which hand the pebble's in, comes with me.'

Much to Patch's dismay, it was Pinch who guessed correctly. She said, 'It's not fair! Why can't we both—'

'Shh,' said Thomas. 'Please, sir,' he went on to the Guardian, 'what do we do next?'

'Come out of thinning. Then the two of you coming here must give the one staying behind one small item of clothing. Anything will do, a handkerchief, a shoelace, a sock. The two of you then select two sticks each. The one who stays must fashion small dolls from these sticks, dress them in the item of clothing, wrap the last grass bracelet around them, and keep the dolls safe all the time you're away. This will enable you to return to your own world safely. You must also all watch that the grass does not start withering. If it does, you must leave at once, no matter what. Do you understand?'

'Oh yes,' said the children, scrambling out of thinning. They picked up some sticks under the willow tree; Thomas gave Patch a sock, Pinch, a bit of material hastily torn off his shirt. As they did so, suddenly they heard voices coming towards them, a commotion further up the river.

'They've found out we've gone!' exclaimed Thomas. 'Quick, sir, what do we do now?'

'Turn to me. Put a hand on each other's shoulders. Close your eyes.'

Thomas and Pinch did as they were told. At once, a cold mist rushed on them, covering them completely, filling their eyes, their ears, their mouths, rushing in like ice water down their throats. They couldn't see each other, or feel anything but thick freezing mist that

turned into vile, smelly fog in an instant. A terrible shrieking filled their ears, shrieking that rose up and up and up till they thought their ears would explode. Then suddenly, they were seized by a wind that rushed at them like a demon, and sent them, blinded, deafened and helpless, spinning through what seemed like endless, cold, white space.

Patch, alone under the big willow, suddenly saw the boys disappear, as if they'd been pulled through a hole in space. In the next instant, the Island of Ghosts itself vanished from the middle of the river, sucked through a funnel of black water that had suddenly appeared in the shining surface of the Riddle. In the instant after that, she heard the sound of raised voices as the adults came crashing down the river bank towards her. But they hadn't seen her yet. Quickly, pocketing sticks, sock and scrap of material, she ran away in the opposite direction. Somehow, she'd have to try and keep out of everyone's way till sunset, she thought. She couldn't afford anyone asking questions or trying to stop Thomas and Pinch from doing what they'd set out to do. And so she started off towards the wood. Her father, the Green Man, had a hideout there. She would make the dolls and stay there till it was time to come back to the river.

SIX

It was cold. Oh, so very cold! Thomas hugged himself, trying to stay warm. The mist still covered him, but it was fading, and now he began to see where he was. He was lying on sand in a huge, round cave. A huge, round, *empty* cave. There was no sign of Pinch, or of the Guardian, or anyone else. He was quite alone. It was very quiet.

'Hello?' he said, sitting up. The last of the mist vanished and he saw that there was an opening down one end of the cave. It was dark, rather ominous, like a gaping, toothless mouth. But it seemed the only way out of here. He got to his feet, a little unsteadily.

'Hello? Anyone there?'

Was that a tiny rustle? It came from the cave mouth.

'Please, who's there? Pinch, where are you?'

Silence.

'Oh well, then,' said Thomas, speaking aloud to make himself feel better, 'I'm going to go and find you, then. You've got to be somewhere here.'

He walked to the opening. Beyond it was a narrow tunnel with a low roof. He took a deep breath. He hated being in tight, dark places. But there was no other way out of the cave. And he had to find Pinch.

He walked into the tunnel. At once, it seemed to get narrower, darker, tighter. He walked a little further, and the tunnel grew so small he was forced to get down on his hands and knees. He thought, I'll go back, I can't stand this, but when he looked over his shoulder, the cave had disappeared and everything was in darkness! He had to go on. There was no other way.

The tunnel got smaller and smaller. Soon he was on his belly, crawling along like a worm. All at once, without any warning, the tunnel dipped steeply down, and he fell through darkness, crying out as he did. He seemed to fall for ages before suddenly being thumped down on what felt like more sand. His heart pounded. Far away, in the distance, he could see a pin-prick of light. He must get there!

He began to crawl along the new tunnel. It was almost as dark and narrow as the other, but rougher. He could feel sharp edges on his hands and his knees. And it was very cold. His teeth were chattering, his whole body shaking with the cold. And then he heard the rustle again . . . and a second later, two red eyes, glowing in the darkness only a short distance from his face. He screamed, and the scream was caught and muffled by the narrow tunnel.

The red eyes winked out. The rustle stopped. 'Mum, Mum,' whispered Thomas, 'where are you? Help me, please . . . Mum . . . where are you?'

Silence . . . but was that a new sound? The sound of a flute, far away? Thomas decided it was. The sound gave him new hope. 'Mum, please help me get to you . . . please help Pinch too . . .'

Was that his imagination, or was the pinprick of light bigger? Whatever, he got new strength from it. He crawled faster. Was the tunnel getting bigger?

Then – splash! He fell into a pool of what felt like melted ice. Gasping, spluttering, he came up to the surface. The light was getting stronger. He could see the other side of the pool. He swam towards it, and emerged, panting, on to the rocky shore. Beyond was another passageway, more like a corridor, this time, and beyond it, a door. Light glowed around the door. Thomas started towards it . . . and yelled as something sharp nipped painfully at his ankle! The red eyes were down there, and they were matched with some sharp teeth, and pointed ears – it was a rat. A huge rat. Thomas had never liked rats, but he wasn't scared of them. He kicked out at it, hard. 'Go away, you ugly thing!'

To his horror, the rat spoke. 'I am a guide sent to you by the Guardian of the gate,' it said.

'Oops,' said Thomas. 'Sorry. Hope I didn't hurt you.'

The rat laughed. 'Hurt me? How could you? Now I can only take you the next step. You must be careful here. For instance, you were going to go through that door. That is the door of no return. Only the dead may go through there.'

'Oh,' said Thomas, shivering a little. 'Then where do I go? There is no other place.'

'Here,' said the rat, and scuttled up the rough wall of the passageway to a tiny opening.

'You must be joking,' said Thomas. 'How can I possibly get through there?'

'Here, you are not as you were,' said the rat. 'You are not solid flesh, but a shadow. That should help you.' In a twinkling, it vanished.

Thomas stood perplexed. 'How can that help me?' he said, looking down at his hands, which seemed, to him, as solid as ever. 'Please tell me, what do I do?'

A voice came booming hollowly into the passage. 'You are a Rymer, son of a Rymer. Use your head!'

'That's all very well,' said Thomas, 'but it doesn't really help me. I need to get smaller, that's what I need.' Still, he began scrambling up the rough wall, trying to find footholds and handholds. Then he noticed something. His hands did seem to be getting smaller! 'I'm a Rymer, son of a Rymer,' he said, aloud. 'I wonder if that means things can happen here if I wish them, or think them? Let's try. I wish I could be small enough to fit down that hole . . .'

Whoosh! The hole seemed to reach out

for him, suck him in, like water going down the plughole. It was an instant before he realised that in fact he *had* shrunk and fallen through the hole. 'Well, that worked, anyway,' he thought, as he crept carefully along yet another dark tunnel. 'I wonder if other wishes will work? Like, I wish I could be with Pinch.'

Nothing happened. But was that the sound of the flute again?

He crept along. He didn't want to fall into any more pools without warning. He was cold enough as it was. On and on, he went, until quite suddenly, the tunnel ended. Faint light showed around the opening. Thomas crawled along to it and looked through, down into an unexpectedly cosy scene.

It was a large, comfortable room. Tall lamps cast a warm golden light all around. On three walls were tall, wooden filing cabinets and long tables cluttered with objects of all sorts: funnels, test tubes, jars, piles of paper, and more. The fourth wall was lined with a big bookshelf stuffed with books that had titles in languages Thomas could not recognise.

Directly below him was a desk, with a thin, tall figure sitting at it, writing in a large book. The figure wore old-fashioned dark robes and a velvet cap on top of silver hair. Thomas couldn't see its face. Just behind the figure was a tall mirror made of a greenish glass. Thomas suddenly saw something in the glass. A shadow, looming; a small, dark shadow, getting closer . . . He leaned forward to see better, but lost his balance and fell through the opening, landing in a heap at the figure's feet. But it did not even look up or seem to notice.

Thomas jumped up – just in time, as the figure got to its feet and lumbered over to one of the tables, narrowly missing Thomas. He picked something up – it looked like a big jar, covered with a piece of cloth – and carried it to the desk. Then he pulled the covering off, and peered inside.

Thomas gasped. It was indeed a big jar. And trapped in it, trying to crawl up the slippery glass walls like a captured insect, was a tiny Pinch!

SEVEN

Bending over the jar, the robed figure spoke for the first time. It was a man's voice, rather fussy, but kind, too. 'Now, then, little Middler, it's no use taking on so. This jar is the best place for you. You're safe, there. Now, let me see, where did I put that magnifying glass . . .'

The hooded figure turned away, looking vaguely around the room. Thomas could see its face now – or rather, the black half-mask where the top of its face should have been. Behind the mask, blue eyes glittered, and the mouth was hidden under a thick silver moustache and beard.

Thomas's heart thumped. He wished he

could get out of here, and fast. But he couldn't leave Pinch here, at the mercy of this weird creature. Who knew what it intended to do to him?

He would have to climb up to the desk without being seen. Maybe he could push the jar so that it overbalanced and broke, and Pinch could get out?

He started climbing up the leg of the desk, carefully. It was rather slippery and he had to push himself hard to keep going. At last, though, he got to the desk top. Pinch, now sitting rather glumly at the bottom of the jar, saw him at once. His eyes widened.

I'll get you out, mimed Thomas. He mimed a push and rolling the bottle. He hoped Pinch would understand. If he ran hard at the side of the jar, he might make it tip over, and then Thomas could push it off the desk. That would be a dangerous moment, for the ghost would be sure to hear the sound of breaking glass. But it was the only thing he could think of.

The jar rocked a little as Pinch ran at the side. Thomas reached up and pushed. But still it didn't fall over. Once more, and they ran again, Thomas pushed, the jar rocked harder this time. One more time might have done it, but at that moment, a hand came down on Thomas and picked him up. Dangling from a bony pair of fingers, kicking and screaming, he was brought up level to the ghost's masked face. The glittering eyes surveyed him.

The ghost spoke. 'I caught sight of you in the shadow-mirror. Another intruder from the living worlds! They're coming from everywhere today. Well, best pop you in the jar too, eh?'

'No! Please listen to me! I'm a Rymer!' Thomas shouted with all his might, knowing that otherwise the ghost would not hear his tiny voice.

'A Rymer? But you're a living one. I can tell, because you're a shadow here, not solid as you ought to be. See?' And he pressed a finger on Thomas's arm, who, to his horror, saw it go right in, as though he were just made of mist. Only the grass bracelet, still dangling on his wrist and still green, looked solid. 'A living Rymer!' said the ghost. 'What are you doing here? You must be crazy. How did you get past the Guardian? What tricks did you use?'

'I didn't,' yelled Thomas. 'He let us in. I'm in

danger, you see. And I've come to find out what from.'

'Easy,' said the ghost. 'I heard that Mister D is on his way to pick up a Rymer. Happens it's you, my lad.'

'Are you sure?' said Thomas, trembling.

'Well, he's expected here today. He always passes through here on his way to do a job, to get the necessary forms and so on from the Guardian. You see, a place for the new ghost-Rymer has to be allocated, if he's been selected to come here.'

'But why . . . why is he after me?'

'Who knows?' shrugged the ghost. 'Mister D's reasons are not easy to understand. Your time may have come, that's all.'

'But I was getting better!' cried Thomas. He felt rather scared, now.

The ghost shrugged again. 'It may not be you he's after, of course. How should I know? There may be other Rymers at present in the Hidden World.'

'I . . . I haven't heard of anyone else,' said Thomas, sadly.

'Never mind, lad,' said the ghost, kindly. 'It's not so bad. You're here already, after all. You won't even have to be taken for the ride here. Once Mister D taps you on the shoulder and those forms are filled in, that'll be it.'

'But I don't want to,' said Thomas. 'I'm not ready to die!' Suddenly, he wished with all his heart that he was out of here. He tried to make the wish come true. But nothing happened. What sort of fool was he, coming here? And it wasn't as though he'd not been warned. Why, oh why, hadn't he done what Dad and Angelica and the others wanted him to do?

The ghost's glittering eyes softened a little. 'Don't take on so,' it said, gently. 'It may not be you he is after. Perhaps someone here might know. I don't, I'm afraid.'

'My mother,' said Thomas, his lips trembling. 'My mother. She's here on this island. She was a Rymer too. She'd be bound to

68

know, wouldn't she, if I . . . if I . . .'

'Perhaps, perhaps,' said the ghost, heartily. 'Mister D isn't one for talking about his business far and wide, or divulging the names of his passengers – but you never know. A mother's heart may pierce even his secrets.'

'Well, then I'm going to go and find her.'

'Without a guide, you won't find her,' said the ghost, shaking his head. 'And you may well meet Mister D and his Riders unexpectedly, if you try on your own.'

'Please, will you help, then? Just to find Mum and speak to her, then I and my friend will be gone, and we'll escape Mister D.'

The ghost laughed, softly. 'I have heard of only a few people who ever escaped Mister D. And that was only because he took someone else in their place.'

'Can you help us?' asked Thomas, stubbornly, trying not to hear what the ghost had said.

'Perhaps,' said the ghost. 'Who is your mother?'

'Her name is Mab Trew.'

The ghost sighed, deeply. 'Ah! I know her. She doesn't wear a mask. That is because she is remembered with great love by the living, you see, and not forgotten.' The voice faltered a little. 'Me, you see, I am forgotten. No one thinks fondly of me, or tells stories about me.' The voice cracked. 'And so, the mask has grown on me – and even my name is lost to me, though I have worked hard to find it again. Ghosts do not eat or sleep or drink or do many things that we once did in life. But the thing we loved doing best of all, this we usually keep in our memory. I know I loved knowledge. I loved learning, finding out things. I think I must have been a scientist, or some such seeker-after-knowledge, as well as a Rymer. But I cannot find out this one thing – my own name. I cannot tell you who exactly I am, for I, too, have forgotten. I am known as Doctor Noname, even to myself.'

Thomas felt a surge of pity. 'I will find out,'

he said, impulsively. 'If you will help us, I'll try and find out who you are, and give you back your name.'

'But there is only one way to do that,' cried the ghost. 'And that is to look in Mister D's files. He will never let you look. Besides, you cannot linger till he comes, or there's no telling what will happen, whether or not it's you he's after.'

'I'll think of something,' said Thomas, trying to sound confident. 'Please, let my friend out, take us to my mother, and I promise I will find out, somehow, who you are. And I'll tell everyone I know about you, and then people will remember you, and know who you are.'

'You promise?' said the ghost, eagerly. 'Really? You promise, on your own name?'

'Really,' said Thomas. 'I promise on my own name, Thomas Trew.'

'Then I will help you, Thomas Trew,' cried Doctor Noname, and he dropped Thomas back down on the desk. He picked up the jar, uncorked it, and turned it upside down. Yelling as he went, Pinch tumbled helter-skelter down the glass walls and popped out of the opening, landing with a jolt on the desk top.

'You could have been more careful,' he huffed, glaring up at the ghost. 'And what do you mean by putting me in a jar like a fly?'

'This is Doctor Noname. He's going to help us,' said Thomas, hurriedly. 'Doctor, please meet my friend, Pinch Gull.'

'Pleased to meet you,' said the ghost.

Pinch said, gruffly, 'Hello.'

Thomas explained, 'He's going to take us to Mum. And then we'll go, because Mister D is on his way and we don't want to meet him.' He spoke jauntily, but Pinch saw his expression.

'I'm sure he hasn't come looking for you,' he said stoutly. 'I'm sure of that!'

'So am I,' said Thomas, more confidently than he felt. 'But I have to talk to Mum, quickly, and find out the truth.'

'That is, if we can find Mab quickly. She

does tend to wander, you know,' said the Doctor. Despite the gloomy words, he sounded cheerful again, and his eyes sparkled, as if he was looking forward to their task. 'Anyway . . .' and before anyone could say or do anything, he reached down and picked the two of them up, and shoved them in his big front pocket. 'Best to keep you out of sight, just in case.'

EIGHT

Patch got to her father's hideout in the wood only to discover he wasn't at home. And neither were any of his friends. His home, deep within a hollow tree, was shut up and she was unable to get in. What should she do now? Sit on her father's doorstep till he came home? Go off looking for him in the depths of the wood? He often went hunting. But she didn't feel very sure about the wood. She did have greenwood blood herself, but she lived in Owlchurch. The riverside was more her thing. But she couldn't go back there, not yet, or she'd be found and made to tell what she knew. She had no doubt that the others could get Thomas and Pinch back and send Thomas packing back to London, before he could find out anything at all.

So she sat on the doorstep and put the dolls together. Patch was clever with her hands and the dolls looked good. As well as the sticks, the sock and the scrap of Pinch's shirt, she used bits of straw, bright leaves and flowers. For faces, she used big leaves, and little pebbles for the eyes, nose and mouth. Next, she put the grass bracelet around them and glamoured the whole thing so that it hung together and wouldn't come apart.

Patch felt quite hurt that she, who was the first person to see the island and to hear the Guardian's first words, was the one left behind. Like Pinch, she went with Thomas on all his adventures. But she'd gone one time when Pinch hadn't, in the Uncouthers' country. And she thought that sometimes she knew more than Pinch did. He did rush things sometimes. She felt sure Thomas would have been better off with her.

Brooding, she settled back against the tree, the dolls near her. Shortly, she began to feel tired. Very tired. She'd been up really early, after all, and a lot of things had already happened. She looked up at the sun shining through the leaves. It was not long after midday – well, closer to early afternoon. It might be hours before the others got back, she thought. She could have a little nap till her father returned, anyway. She closed her eyes and in a few seconds was asleep.

She woke suddenly. There was a noise, close by. A rustling noise, coming closer. Her father, returning? No, it didn't sound like him. He marched through the wood, jauntily, and his friends sang as they walked. An animal, then? There were unicorns that roamed these woods, and they could be very bad-tempered. It might even be something worse . . . Taking sudden fright at these thoughts and forgetting all about the dolls, she clambered up into the tree's leafy top and peered down.

There was definitely something moving to one side of the path, in a wild patch of tangled bushes. She could hear the rustling of bushes and the cracking of twigs. It sounded quite big and blundering about, as if it was scared or angry. Patch hugged herself. She would stay here till the thing, whatever it was, had gone away.

It was then she remembered the dolls. Oh no! she thought. What an idiot I am! What if that thing finds them and messes them up, or worse still, eats them! Then Thomas and Pinch will be in desperate trouble! She couldn't stay up here. She had to get down and save the dolls. Her skin crawled as she climbed silently down, but she kept going, bravely. She would just snatch them up, quickly, put them in her pocket and race up the tree again.

She reached the bottom without trouble. The thing was still crashing and blundering about in the bushes. Then, just as she bent down to pick up the dolls, she heard a voice, clearly, saying, 'Ow!'

She jumped back and stared at the dolls, for one moment thinking one of them had spoken. Then the voice spoke again. 'Ow! Stupid thing!'

It was a girl's voice. It was coming from within those bushes. Cautiously, her eyes narrowed, Patch crept towards them. Now she began to see a little more clearly. Someone was caught up in the tangled branches and thorns of the bushes and was struggling to get out. But Patch knew that wouldn't be easy. That's because those bushes were tightening around the person, like a trap. And that could only be because the person was an intruder who didn't belong here and had no business to be here. It must be someone who came from somewhere far away, and didn't understand how things worked here.

'You'd better stop struggling,' Patch said, clearly. 'Or the bushes will end up choking you.'

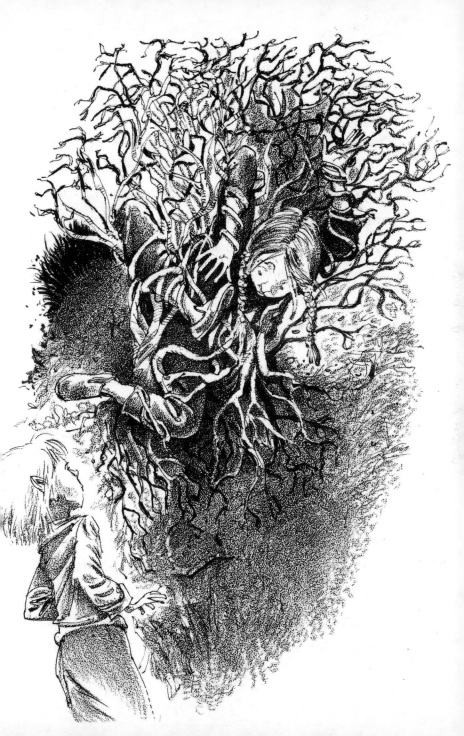

The struggling stopped for an instant. A scared voice said, 'Who's that?'

'Me,' said Patch, carefully. She didn't want to give her name, not yet, not till she knew who this person was and what had happened. 'Who are you? And why are you here?'

'I'm Alice,' said the girl. 'Alice Grimm. And I'm here because I followed my uncle.' There was a pause, then Alice said, 'I don't even know where I am. How far is this from London?'

'London!' cried Patch. 'You mean, you're an Obbo?'

'What's that?' said the girl.

'Someone from the Obvious World. You're in the Hidden World,' said Patch, excitedly, 'in my father's wood. Where's your uncle and what's going on?'

'I don't know,' said the girl. 'Look, can you get me out of here? It's awfully uncomfortable.'

'Wait a moment,' said Patch, and racked her brains to think of a simple spell that would make the bushes lose their grip. At last, she remembered one and gabbled the words.

The branches fell back and a girl emerged from the bushes. She was about Patch's size, with a bright face, brown eyes and fair hair in two plaits. She looked hot and tired. There were scratches from the briars on her arms and legs. She blinked at Patch. 'Oh, hello.'

'Are you all right?' asked Patch.

'I think so.' Alice stared at Patch, then at the tree. 'Is this really your father's wood?'

'Well, he lives here,' Patch answered. 'He's the Green Man, you see. He's an outlaw and he roams here with his gang.'

'Really?' Alice's eyes widered. 'Do you live here with him too?'

'Oh, no. I live in Owlchurch, with my brother and my mother . . .' She broke off, staring at Alice, suspiciously. 'You're from London? You know Thomas, then? Is that why you're here?'

'What?' said Alice. 'Who's Thomas?'

'Thomas Trew. He's a Rymer.'

'What's that? And I never heard of a Thomas Trew,' said Alice. She smiled. 'London's very big, you know. But I think I've heard of a Hidden World. I mean, I've always imagined there'd be one. Are you magic? Am I in a dream?'

Patch stared at her, nonplussed. 'Don't be silly. This is real. And I'm not magic. I'm just Patch.'

'Patch,' said the girl, thoughtfully. 'What's that? Oh, I see – your name.'

'Of course, silly,' said Patch. 'What did you think it was?'

'Will you disappear if I close my eyes?' said Alice.

Patch glared at her. 'Oh, you are too silly for words,' she said, huffily, and stalked off to pick up the dolls. Alice followed her.

'What are you doing? What's that?'

'What do you think?' said Patch, crossly.

'Sort of dolls . . . Can we play with them?'

'Certainly not! They're very important.

They're dolls of my friend Thomas and my brother Pinch, and if I don't take care of them, they'll never come back.'

'Ooh,' said Alice, eagerly. 'Come back from where?'

Patch was about to tell her, then thought better of it. 'Never mind.'

'What are we going to do now?' said Alice.

'What do you mean? You're going to have to find your uncle and get back to your own world before anyone else finds you. Does your uncle have permission to be here? He's a wizard, I suppose, is he?'

'I suppose so,' said Alice. 'I mean, lately he's always mucking about with spells and potions and things, but he's not been really good at it till now. He's tried all sorts of things, you see. He used to write books, but no one read them; and then he painted pictures, but nobody liked them; and then he tried to write songs and no one wanted to listen to them. So he decided he'd try magic instead. He said he could make people do just what he wanted, then. He's really, really not a very nice person,' she said, in a burst of confidence. 'He said he'd turn me into a bat or a toad if I didn't stop annoying him. I don't think he can do that, really, but you never know. You see, he's looking after me – or he's supposed to – because my parents died in an accident a year ago, and he's my father's younger brother, but he's nothing like Dad. I don't much like living with him, except for the wizarding bit. I think I could be quite good at it, but he won't let me try, of course.'

'Oh,' said Patch, a bit stunned by this flow of words. 'Well, I don't remember anyone saying a wizard was going to visit here.'

'I don't suppose Uncle Jim asked. He's like that. He crashes parties and he steals things and eats other people's lunches, and that sort of thing.'

'He doesn't sound at all nice,' said Patch. 'So he came in without permission. But he must have had help from someone. Who from? And how did you get in here?'

'I told you, I followed him,' said Alice. 'He told me this morning I was not to disturb him, that I was to stay in my room all day. In fact, he even locked me in! But after a little while I managed to climb out of the window and I crept back into the house through the laundry window . . . and I saw him in this study with these two strangers. They were giving him something – a bottle filled with something green. Well, then they left – though I didn't see how, unless they flew out of the window or something . . . Then Uncle Jim drank the green liquid and he vanished! I couldn't believe my eyes! I went into the study and I saw there were some drops of that potion left in the bottle, so I thought I'd drink it and see what happened and what he was up to. And suddenly I found myself in this place and those horrid bushes tried to strangle me . . .'

'They're not horrid,' said Patch, sternly.

'They just guard against intruders. What did those people look like, with your uncle?'

'Couldn't see properly,' said Alice. 'They were all wrapped up in black cloaks or something. One was tall, the other short, that's all I really saw.'

'Where's your uncle now?'

'I don't know,' said Alice.

'I suppose if you're here, he's got to be somewhere around here too.' That wasn't a nice thought, really – some crooked wizard lurking about. 'Oh dear, I wish Father was here.'

'He won't be back till nightfall,' said a gruff voice suddenly, startling them. Alice stared when she saw who had spoken, for it was a person who looked rather like a walking, talking bush. But Patch was very relieved. 'Am I ever glad to see you, Skrob!' she said.

'Really?' said Skrob, suspiciously, looking from one girl to the other. 'What's going on, Patch? And who's this?'

NINE

The corridor outside the ghost's room was very long and glowed white and silver. On its walls were framed pictures of landscapes. But as they got closer to each one, the scene in the picture misted over and disappeared, so that you could never quite tell what they looked like.

As they walked along, Thomas and Pinch in Doctor Noname's pocket, the ghost told them a little about the strange world of the island. Not all Rymers came here, he said, you had to be selected. Wicked Rymers were not allowed in, for instance. When Thomas asked if the first Rymer was here, Doctor Noname nodded. 'But he's very shy, is True Tom, and keeps himself to himself.' He went on to explain that each ghost created his or her own home, based on their favourite dream place. Ghosts here spent their time doing what they'd loved best in life, and did not return to the Obvious World. The island was a good, peaceful and pleasant place, he said. It would last in peace till the end of the world.

They reached a door down the end of the corridor. As the ghost opened it, Thomas gasped. For here was the exact scene of his weird dream. There was a giant merry-go-round, with carriages like large acorn cups dangling from the middle, on thin silver wires.

The ghost said, 'This is our shuttle service. You see, the island is like a series of little worlds, each created by an individual Rymer, and you can only travel between them this way.' He clambered into a carriage. 'Right, now hold on tight. It's a bit abrupt, at first.'

He touched one of the wires. 'To Mab's world,' he shouted, and all at once, the merry-

go-round started
to move. Faster
and faster it
went, and the
children had to
cling on to the
pocket with all
their might to stop
themselves from being
flung out. Faster, faster,
faster, and their heads
seemed to be spinning
around. Then, *twang!* went
one of the wires of the
carriage, and the carriage
swung alarmingly out into
space. *Twang!* went another,
and now the boys were
tumbled about in the
bottom of the pocket,
bumping painfully against
each other, yelling and

screaming. *Twang!* went yet another wire, and now the carriage lurched out into emptiness, swinging this way and that, turning them all practically upside down, their fingers scrabbling desperately to cling to the material of the pocket. 'Hold on,' shouted the ghost, as the last wire broke and the carriage plunged like a stone. Then just before it reached the ground, straight up it went again and then settled into a steady, rocking motion. After a short time, they plucked up enough courage to put their heads out of the ghost's pocket again and look down. And there they saw an enchanting sight.

From up here, the island looked like a kind of giant, interlocking jigsaw puzzle, with each piece quite different and very colourful. Here was a white castle, with silver turrets gleaming in the sun, next to a glassy lake; here was an isolated green valley, with a single little house, its chimney smoking; there was a miniature town, with what looked like carved gingerbread houses and tiny little shops; there again was an expanse of wild, rocky heather, and a thatched house, hidden behind a patch of dense woodland. ('That's the house of the first Rymer,' shouted Doctor Noname, into the wind. 'Like I told you, he doesn't like visitors; that wood is enchanted, and you wouldn't want to fall in there.') There was a kind of reed-house floating on a blue lake, and further away a golden-domed palace, with neat gardens all around it. There was more, much more, and as they flew over it all, the boys half forgot that they were on a mission.

All at once, the carriage plunged down again, very quickly – so quickly they could not see or hear or think. Thomas's head filled with whizzing air and his nose and throat burned. Another lurch, a hiss, and then all at once the carriage sped down again and landed with a jolt. With a last wild yell, the boys flew out of the ghost's pocket, on to what seemed to be soft, green grass.

After an instant, Thomas cautiously opened his streaming eyes. It *was* soft, green grass he was lying on. They were in a meadow. A beautiful, peaceful meadow, filled with flowers and birdsong and sunlight. There was a cluster of blossom trees down one end and a little river ran beside them. Then he looked down at himself and saw that he was his proper size again, yet he was just as shadowy as ever, except for the grass bracelet. He peered at it. Was it his imagination, or had the green started fading a little?

He looked for Pinch. The Middler boy was getting slowly to his feet. He, too, was back to his normal size, but he had become transparent – Thomas could see the field through his body. To Thomas's relief, the grass bracelet on Pinch's wrist still looked bright green. I must be imagining things, he thought.

'A most fine day, is it not?' said the ghost, startling them both. Thomas had a funny feeling, then, as if the way the ghost had said those words was familiar. The ghost went on, 'These are the Pleasant Fields. Mab's world. One of the nicest homes in all the island, after mine, of course. She'll be somewhere here.' He stopped, and cupped a hand to where his ear would be, if it could be seen. 'Actually, I think I hear her flute. Can you?'

Thomas strained his ears, but could hear nothing, though his heart beat so fast he thought it must jump through his chest and up his throat into his mouth. 'No,' he said, sadly.

'Then come with me,' said the ghost, gliding off rapidly through the soft, flowery grass, with Thomas and Pinch racing to keep up.

Under the trees, it was lovely and quiet, the pink and white blossom falling like scented snow on them. But there was no Mab Trew to be seen. No one at all, in fact.

'Dear me, I could have sworn . . .' said Doctor Noname, and cocked his head, listening. 'Hmm. I think it's further on . . .' and he was off.

Past the trees, and now they were in another meadow. It was quite full of bright little blue flowers that looked for all the world like tiny stars come to earth, and the grass was silver, not green. At one end of it, they could see a beautiful little white house, with a roof that glittered gold. Doctor Noname turned to them, his face radiant. 'She's there. Look at all the butterflies . . .'

And indeed the air around the house was quite thick with what Thomas had taken at first to be a low cloud – but a rainbow cloud, made up of all sorts of colours. Now he saw they were tiny butterflies, hovering. And in the same instant, he heard a sound. It grew into more sound. A tune. He knew the tune! It was the tune she'd played when he had escaped from Nightmare, the Uncouthers' country. It was the song of the Rymer. In the next moment, he saw, sitting half hidden amongst the cloud of butterflies, a figure he knew well . . .

'Mum!' he cried, and ran through the silver grass, that clinked and sparkled as he ran as if it was made of glass.

She was small, and slender, with a wild bush of black hair, and a pale face, and eyes the same colour as Thomas's own. She looked like the photograph they had hanging in the living room in London, except she was more beautiful even than that. She was dressed in a pale yellow dress, and on her head was a little crown made of those blue meadow flowers. Her feet were bare, and she had her flute to her lips. She looked very young, much too young to be Thomas's mother. Butterflies fluttered all around her, lighting on her head, her shoulders, her flute. Thomas couldn't stop looking at her, and he couldn't move, or speak.

She said, very gently, 'Thomas,' and then he found he could move, and he ran straight into her arms, forgetting he was but a shadow here. But his mother held him tight, and though he was still a shadow, it seemed to him he could feel her touch, as solid and warm as in life.

'Oh, Mum, I've missed you; I've missed you so much,' he cried. 'I can't tell you how much.'

'Hush. I know,' she said, stroking his hair.

Before he saw her, Thomas had intended to ask her to help him find out what was happening, but now other words flew into his mouth. 'Oh, Mum, please, won't you come back with me? Please, I miss you so much . . .

and Dad does too . . . and we want you back . . . oh, we so want you back.'

'My darling,' she said, and her voice trembled. 'I can't.'

'But why not? Why not? You're a great Rymer . . . and you helped me, twice . . . I saw you, I really did . . . and so it must be different for you than for others . . . You must be allowed to come back . . .'

'I'm lucky,' she said, quietly. 'I'm still loved. I can come back . . . in dreams, in visions – but not in the flesh. Once Mister D has written your name in his files, there is nothing you can do to change that.'

'Who says?' said Thomas, fiercely, hot tears choking him.

'It is the law of the world,' said his mother, gently, holding him. 'It is the law of all of us humans, Rymer or not Rymer. But one day – one day we will be together again.'

Thomas couldn't help shivering. But maybe, he thought, dying wouldn't be so bad, if he could be with his mother, in this lovely place . . .

'What's wrong, Thomas?' she said, gently.

'It's Mister D,' said the doctor, speaking for the first time. 'He's on his way. And I have heard it is to pick up a Rymer.'

'No,' said Mab. 'Oh no. It is not Thomas's time. Not yet. Surely not – I would have heard. I would know, if it was Thomas. There are many Rymers in the world, many.'

Doctor Noname said, sadly, 'The island appeared to them, dear lady. The Guardian said there was danger, to the Rymer.'

'Danger,' said Mab Trew. 'That may mean many things, and not just Mister D. Danger does not mean a certainty of death. But when the island appears, it is a serious warning of danger – in the Hidden World, and never in the Obvious World. The warnings there are different. Well! It is clear what must be done. Thomas, you must go back to London.'

'Oh no, Mum. Not you too!' Thomas

beckoned Pinch forward. 'Mum, this is one of my best friends, Pinch Gull. His twin sister Patch is my other best friend. And they're why I don't want to go back to the Obvious World. I don't have good friends like them in London. In fact, I don't have any friends. You're not there, it's grey and dull, and there's no magic and no adventures, and besides what's to stop Mister D from following me there, if it's me he wants?'

'I told you, I'm sure it's not you he's after,' said his mother. 'There may be other Rymers in the Hidden World.'

'I haven't heard of any others,' said Thomas, but Pinch broke in.

'There may be one somewhere we haven't heard of,' he said. 'There's lots of parts of the Hidden World, not just Owlchurch. Maybe there's a Rymer staying with the Montaynards, or the Seafolk, or the Ariels, or even with the Uncouthers.'

'In any case, Thomas, any danger to you is in

the Hidden World. Not the Obvious World. That is why you must return there, at once.' She went on, thoughtfully, 'But it does seem odd. You were in the most danger ever in Ariel country. And yet the island did not appear before you went there. Now you should be safe. But perhaps the poison from the Flying Huntsman's arrow has struck deep inside you, too deep for healing in the world that caused it. It could be killing you slowly. I have heard of these things happening before.'

'But I feel fine,' said Thomas. 'I *am* fine!'

Mab Trew shook her head. 'If Angelica and all the others – who have great powers of understanding – say that you must go back to London, then go back you must. It is not safe for you in the Hidden World any more, my darling, and you must understand that I think they were right – that is where the danger is for you. Once out of it, you will be safe – from Mister D and all other dangers.'

'So all I have to do is just do what they say

and go back to London?' said Thomas, dismayed.

His mother sighed. 'I know, Thomas, it is disappointing, and especially after everything else that has happened to you, and all the adventures. But it is a fact.' She looked at Pinch's downcast face. 'I am sure it can be arranged for you to visit Thomas quite often.'

'That's not the same as being in the same village,' said Thomas, crossly.

'No. But it's better than nothing.'

'But, Mum . . . what about you? If I . . . if I really have to go back to London, then I'll never see you again in my life, will I? Not really, to talk to, like this . . . or even to hear you, like I did in Nightmare and in the Ariel country . . .'

'No,' said Mab, very quietly. 'Not unless I came back – oh, not as a living person, that's impossible. But there is another . . . another possibility. I can break out of this world and return as a homeless ghost, haunting her own old home. I will do that, Thomas, if that is truly what you want. What you need. But it will frighten your father, and hurt him, and all his chances of living normally again. For there is a chance for him, isn't there? A girl he is beginning to love?'

'That Lily,' said Thomas, fiercely. 'She thinks she can take your place. She can't!'

'I'm sure she doesn't want to,' said Mab, smiling gently. 'I'm sure that's not what Gareth wants, either. But he is alive, and he is a kind, loving man. He should not have to live only with a memory for the rest of his life.'

'I don't know how he can forget you,' Thomas cried.

'He doesn't, my darling. As neither do I forget him. But we cannot go back to what was.'

'But you said you would come back if I wanted you to,' said Thomas desperately.

'Yes. But only as a homeless ghost,' she said, sadly.

'Don't ask that!' cried Doctor Noname. 'It is

what we are most afraid of, all of us here. In your world she will be a dismal shadow. She will never be at peace again. She will be racked with pain and hopeless longing. She will frighten the man who once loved her, and he will flee from her in terror and horror. She will be homeless for ever, till the end of the world. What's more, one day you will forget her, and it will be like a second death, and more suffering still. And you will never be together again, not till the end of the world.'

'Doctor Noname,' said Mab Trew, angrily, 'I did not ask you to say such things. You should not speak for others.'

Thomas was very pale. 'But is it true, Mum? Are all those things true? Please, tell me.'

'I would bear them if you wanted me to,' said Mab, quietly.

'It's not fair,' said Thomas, very low. 'All I want to do is stay in the Hidden World . . . where I can be with my friends – where I can be much closer to you, too. But I can't. I have to go back to a world I don't care about any more, where I have no friends. And where I . . . where I can't see you like I do in the Hidden World . . . It's not fair. It's not fair!'

'Then I will go with you as a haunting ghost,' said Mab, sadly.

'No,' said Thomas, though his heart felt like it would break in two. 'No, Mum. I . . . I couldn't bear to think you'd be in pain . . . I . . . I'd much rather think of you happy and at peace here, and that one day, I . . . I will see you again.' He swallowed. 'And maybe . . . later . . . when I'm allowed to go back to the Hidden World, will you come to me, when I call on you?'

'Of course,' she said, gently. 'I watch over you, darling Thomas, and I'll never stop doing that, wherever in the worlds you may be. In the Hidden World I can speak with you – but in the Obvious World I will be there in your dreams and your memory. I promise.' She gave a deep sigh. 'And now, Thomas, you should go.'

'But we've only just arrived! Can't we stay a tiny, tiny bit longer?' begged Thomas. 'Just a tiny bit?' He held up his wrist to her. 'Look, the bracelet's still green. We're still OK.'

'Very well,' she said. 'And I'll give you a song to go with you, my darling, to help you through all the hard times ahead . . .'

Then Thomas's mother put the flute to her lips and began to play. It was a beautiful tune, the most beautiful one Thomas had ever heard. Sweet, soft, a little sad, yet with a joyous trill of notes, it made him want to both laugh and cry at the same time. It was a song that expressed all his mother's love, her longing, her hopes for him, her sadness at their parting but her happiness at having been allowed to hold him again, this one time.

Pinch and Doctor Noname listened too. It seemed to speak differently to them, for as the last notes died away, Pinch whispered, 'Thomas . . . that song says we'll always be friends, no matter what happens.'

Thomas's throat felt tight. He whispered, 'Yes. Yes we will,' and he wished with all his heart, all his mind, all his soul, that things were different.

There was a little gulp. Doctor Noname had his hands up to his masked face, and his shoulders shook with sobs. 'Oh, now I understand why they remember you,' he cried. 'But what of me? I am nobody, and nothing, and will be till the end of time.'

'I promised him I'd find out his name, I'd look in Mister D's files,' said Thomas to his mother.

She gasped. 'Impossible!' She turned to Noname. 'You should have known better than to ask for that!'

'He didn't,' began Thomas, but the doctor interrupted. 'She's right. You cannot find out my name,' he wept. 'You cannot. It is too dangerous, and I do not deserve it. I think I must not have been a very good person in life for no one to care about me. And I do not want you to risk meeting Mister D. Your mother is right. You must go.'

'Oh, but . . .' Thomas began, when his mother put a finger to her lips. She picked up her flute again and began to play. But though Thomas and the twins heard nothing, clearly that was not the case for the Doctor. After a moment, he lifted his head up and sat there, listening, and then began to sway, gently, like a tree bending in the wind. Then he began to hum, gently at first, then louder.

At last, Mab took the flute from her lips, but still the nameless ghost kept humming. Then, still humming happily, he got to his feet and blundered away through the meadow, picking flowers as he went.

'He'll be all right, now,' said Mab Trew, to the boys. 'Don't feel too sad for him. He is happy most of the time, it's only when he remembers about forgetting who he was that he gets upset.'

'But I feel bad,' said Thomas. 'I promised to help, and I haven't kept my promise.'

'He knows it was a promise you couldn't keep,' said his mother.

'But it seems sad that no one cares about him,' said Thomas.

'Well, you see, he probably died a very, very long time ago. There's no one left to remember.'

'Oh,' said Thomas, feeling suddenly a little cold.

His mother hugged him, then stood up. 'Come, all of you. It's time I took you back to the Guardian and . . .' She broke off, frowning. 'What's that noise?' Then her face changed, and she scrambled up. 'Quick! In the house and don't come out till I tell you to. You'll be safe there, my love will block you from his sight.'

TEN

As soon as he heard what had happened, Skrob suggested he'd take a message down to the village. He promised not to mention Patch's name. He didn't need to, he said. After all, he was part of the Green Man's gang, an outlaw, always running around the woods. It was quite believable he might find a strange human girl wandering around. Meanwhile, he said, he'd open up the Green Man's house, and Alice and Patch should wait there till he returned. As to Thomas and Pinch, 'Well,' he said, sternly, but with a twinkle in his eye, 'those two rascals have really done it this time. If they get out of this one, they'll be in hot water with Angelica and the rest!' He did not sound too worried. He and the rest of the Green Man's gang had always done what they wanted, and they lived by different rules from the people of Owlchurch. 'Now, the other thing,' he said to Alice. 'Tell me what your uncle looks like. If I find him on the way, I'll haul him in for questioning.'

'He's tall and thin, black-haired with a big silver lock flopping on his forehead,' she said, promptly, 'and pale brown eyes and a little moustache. Oh, and he's dressed smartly. In fact he thinks he's very smart. He thinks he's the smartest man who ever lived, in every way. He'll be very rude to you. He's rude to everyone. I think he thinks he should be the king of the world, or something.'

'Well, well, he does sound a most pleasant fellow,' grinned Skrob. 'Let's hope we find him quickly, eh, before he stirs up trouble here. Coming on top of Thomas's and Pinch's escapade, I think this will make Angelica hopping mad. Watch out for fireworks!' As he spoke, he put his hand on the tree trunk and rapped several times, as he were tapping in some code. Then he pressed his thumb against the bark and, all at once, the tree swung open, revealing a passageway beyond. He said to Patch, 'You know the way. And make yourselves at home. I'll be back when I can – and don't worry, well before sunset.' And he was off, with a cheery wave of his hand.

'Wow,' said Alice, as the girls walked into the Green Man's sitting room. 'This is just so cool! And it's all real, not just a picture in a book or something!'

It *was* a beautiful room, light and bright, with green-and-gold tapestries, carpets and cushions everywhere. They shimmered and rustled and sighed like the leaves of trees. 'Well,' said Patch, pleased, 'my father only has the best, you know.'

'Lucky him. Lucky you,' said Alice, throwing

herself on one of the cushions. 'Gosh, I'm tired, all of a sudden. And hungry. You don't think there's anything I could eat, do you? I mean, something that's OK for a human? I mean, you're not a human, are you? You're a fairy or an elf or something. I can tell by those pointed ears.'

'Excuse me,' said Patch, huffily, 'But I'm a Middler, not those things you said.'

'Oh. Sorry,' said Alice. 'Haven't heard of Middlers before.'

'You don't know much,' snapped Patch.

Alice shrugged, and grinned. 'I suppose that's right,' she said, cheerfully. 'But listen, do you think there might be something to eat?'

'There might,' said Patch, sharply. 'Oh, OK! I'll go and see.'

'Thanks a heap,' said Alice, and lay back on the cushions.

Muttering to herself, Patch left the room, and headed to her father's larder. She rummaged around. There was a seed-cake, and some mushroom soup, and boxes of windfall apples and a jar of cider, as well as one of lemonade. She put some slices of seed-cake and some apples and two glasses of lemonade on a tray, and went back to the sitting room – then nearly dropped the tray. For Alice, bolt upright, was staring into a corner of the room, as if she was turned to stone. Patch stared at the corner too. There was nothing there but a tapestry, a rather nice one of a hunting scene. She came in and put down the tray and said, 'What's up with you? You look like you've seen a ghost.' As soon as she said it, she thought of Thomas and Pinch over in that ghostly place, and her heart beat fast. She hoped they were OK, and that they would be back soon, and that everything would be all right.

Alice shook herself. 'Sorry. It was . . . nothing. I thought I saw something . . . someone . . . Must have imagined it. Oh, yummy – cake and apples! My favourite things!'

'Who did you think you saw?' asked Patch,

as they sat and munched.

'Uncle Jim, peeking behind a tree in that picture.'

Patch's skin crept. She looked quickly at the picture again, but there was no sign of the man Alice had described earlier. 'You must have imagined it.'

'Yep,' said Alice, her mouth full of cake. 'Patch, is this magic cake? Is it going to make me go smaller, or turn me into a frog, or give me great powers?'

Patch stared at her. 'It's just cake. The only magic is that it cooked itself.'

'Oh, cool!' said Alice. 'I'd love that. Cakes that cooked themselves, chores that did themselves, homework that finished itself.'

'Sometimes it doesn't quite turn out how you think it will,' said Patch, smiling despite herself. 'Like, once, my brother, who wants to be a Trickster when he grows up like Hinkypunk Hobthrust – never mind, you might get to meet him later – well, he tried to make a mop that would clean the floor by itself, and it just went crazy and tried to mop everything in sight, all Mother's herbs, and our hair, and our faces, and it escaped outside and mopped everything it could, wetting everything and driving everyone mad till Hinkypunk managed to find a spell that would calm it down!'

'Oh, that's like in *The Sorcerer's Apprentice*. It's a story I read once,' Alice explained.

'I don't know it,' frowned Patch. 'And this was real.'

'Can you do magic tricks, Patch?' said Alice, not at all crushed.

'Not tricks,' said Patch, huffily, 'but real magic. Pishogue, we call it.'

'Will you show me some?'

'Oh, OK,' said Patch, and instantly turned herself into a frog, and then into a flea, then a mouse, then back into Patch.

'Wow!' said Alice, eyes round.

'Watch this,' said Patch, and she took one of

the ribbons from Alice's plaits and she blew on it, glamouring it into a little butterfly that flew round and round the room, before alighting on the end of Alice's hair and turning back into a ribbon.

'Wow!' said Alice again. 'Can you teach me some of that?'

'I can't,' said Patch. 'You're not a Rymer. I'm only allowed to teach a bit of pishogue to Rymers, not to ordinary Obbos.'

'I'm not ordinary,' said Alice. 'I think I have wizarding skills. Might that count?'

'No,' said Patch. 'Wizards and witches have to go to special classes and they have special permits. I would not be allowed to teach them.'

'Then maybe I can become a Rymer,' said Alice. 'Then you can teach me.'

'You can't just become one,' said Patch, shaking her head. 'You're born one. Rymers have great gifts. And one day, someone from the Hidden World comes to tell you you're one, and you can come here then and learn more about what kind of Rymer you are. That's what happened to Thomas. He's a real Rymer.'

'Well, how do you know someone's not going to come and tell me?' said Alice. 'How do you know in fact someone's not come and told me already?'

Patch raised her eyebrows. 'Then you'd have known what a Rymer was, wouldn't you?' she said. 'You just wandered in here by mistake, because you swallowed that potion of your uncle's. That's happened before. Witches and wizards are always getting in by mistake, or sneaking in, like your uncle.' She looked sternly at Alice. 'Why do you think he wanted to come here?'

Alice shrugged. 'Do you think he told me? I suppose he was after some knowledge or power or something. Some useless, stupid thing that he could brag about but that would do nobody any good.'

'He can't be such a useless wizard if he

managed to make a potion that would take him here,' said Patch.

'Oh, I suppose it was those strangers that came to see him,' said Alice, shrugging.

'Yes, I was forgetting them,' said Patch. 'I wonder who they were.'

'Proper wizards, I suppose,' said Alice.

'Yes, but why did they give that potion to him? I mean, had you ever seen them before?'

'I don't think so,' said Alice. 'Though I can't be sure,' she added. 'I mean, I only saw them briefly, and I didn't really see what they looked like. Hey, let's stop talking about my uncle, it's boring and horrid. Let's play a game.'

'What kind of game?' said Patch, cautiously.

'Hide and seek,' said Alice. 'I bet there are lots of good hiding-places here. I always wanted to hide in a real proper hollow fairy tree,' she added.

'It's not a fairy tree, it's my father's tree,' snapped Patch.

'Whatever. But do you want to?'

'I suppose so.' What else was there to do?

'You count to a hundred. I'll hide. OK?' And before Patch could answer, Alice had taken off.

I hate counting, thought Patch. She had a good mind to speed it up magically so that she reached one hundred in the time it took a human to count to five. But Alice wouldn't like it and would complain, probably loudly. So she began to count in the ordinary way. I hope she doesn't go poking around in all of Father's things, she thought, as she reached ten.

She'll be easy to find, she thought, as she reached twenty-five. I know every hiding-place here.

Oh, this is boring, she thought, as she reached fifty.

Hurry, hurry, as she passed sixty . . . seventy . . . eighty . . . ninety . . . 'Coming, ready or not,' she bellowed, and scampered off through the house.

Alice wasn't hiding in a cupboard, or in the big chest in the kitchen, or behind the curtains of her father's bed. She wasn't in the rooms of the other gang members and not in the far sitting room. There was only the cellar, and that was a dismal, dank place that Patch didn't like much. But Alice wasn't anywhere else. She had to try there.

Down the stairs she went. The cellar was almost dark, but with a faint greenish light hovering around. That was always there. It was some kind of living lamp Father kept. She peered around. 'Alice?' she said, softly. 'Are you there?'

No answer. Patch moved deeper into the cellar, feeling the hair rising on the back of her neck as she did so. 'Alice?' she called, looking behind the chests, the racks of old bottles. No one. There was a wardrobe down the far end, a great big thing looming black and square against the light. She must be in there. Patch crept over to the wardrobe and tried the door. The handle was stuck. 'Alice!' she said. 'I know you're in there!'

She pulled at the handle and, all of a sudden, it came away in her hand and the door swung open. And there was frightened, pop-eyed Alice, held tight against the chest of a tall, thin man, with a bright lock of silver hair shining on his forehead, strange against the blackness of the rest of his hair. One of the man's hands was on her mouth, to stop her from screaming; the other gripped her tightly.

'No, little one, don't even think about running,' said the man, in a conceited sort of voice. He said a few words, rapidly, under his breath. And to Patch's horror, it seemed as if her feet took root in the cellar floor and her body turned to a block of stone, and all she could do was stand there and stare as Alice's uncle carefully stepped out of the wardrobe, dragging the girl with him.

ELEVEN

In the house, Thomas and Pinch crouched under a low windowsill. They could hear the noise too, now. It was a kind of long, low growl, getting louder and louder by the second, till it became a deafening roar.

'Oh dear, oh dear,' whispered Pinch. He looked grey and frightened.

Thomas was scared too, but he was also curious. Very carefully, he raised his head so he could just see out of the window without being seen.

'What are you doing?' cried Pinch.

Thomas didn't answer. He was too busy looking. His mother was standing in the meadow, one hand up to stop the motorcade coming towards her, loud, slow and very close. In the middle was a great big silver car with white fins and black-tinted windows. There was a plain black flag flying from the grille of the car. Before the car came two riders on huge motorbikes, one red, one black; and behind it were two riders on huge motorbikes, one yellow, one white. The riders were gigantic, too, and dressed from head to toe in leather the same colour as their bikes.

'Oh, no,' moaned Pinch, who had quickly stuck his head up and as quickly put it down again. 'I knew it was them. I knew it. What does your mother think she's doing?'

'Is it Mister D and his Riders?' said Thomas.

'Yes. Shh,' said Pinch, his eyes nearly popping out of his head. 'They'll hear you.'

The motorcade stopped. The Riders dismounted. Two of them – the one in yellow and the one in white – went to stand guard by the car. The red Rider walked over to Mab Trew and stood by her, unmoving. The fourth, the black-clad Rider, went over to the car door.

Thomas's skin crept. All four Riders walked stiffly, jerkily, like robots. And now, as they turned, he could see their faces. *Or lack of faces.* Under the leather helmets, the faces were perfectly blank, with no features at all.

The black-clad Rider opened the door wide. Pinch cried, 'Don't look at him, Thomas. Don't look!' But Thomas could not stop looking. He felt as though he were pinned to the spot, staring, as Mister D emerged from his car. Whatever he'd expected, it wasn't this.

Mister D looked like a taller, younger relative of Morph Onery. He was broad, powerful-looking and black-skinned, with a shining mane of pure white hair. But he was dressed much more flashily than Morph, in a pale green silk suit, a green top hat, masses of gold chains, and rings on every finger. He wore green-and-white pointy-toed shoes, and big black glasses sat like insects on his beak of a nose. He wore a thin moustache over thin

lips, and carried a gold-topped cane. As Thomas watched, the black Rider took his arm and guided him towards Mab.

'Oh gosh,' whispered Thomas, suddenly understanding. 'He's blind!'

'Didn't you even know that?' said Pinch, trembling like a leaf. He wasn't looking out of the window but crouching in a corner with his head in his hands.

'Then he can't see me,' said Thomas, defiantly, standing up a bit more to see better.

'Stop that,' hissed Pinch. 'He can sense you, silly. Get down. Oh, dear. I wish we hadn't come here. I wish—'

'You stop it yourself, Pinch,' said Thomas, crossly, watching as Mister D slowly began to make his way to Mab. Then, quite suddenly, he heard his mother's voice in his head. 'Listen carefully, Thomas. Now Mister D is here, your grass bracelets are going to wither very fast . . .' Thomas shot a look at his wrist, and it was true, the green was rapidly turning to yellow.

'You have to get away at once. I'm going to delay Mister D. He gets lonely and is glad of a chat, for his Riders don't talk, humans flee him, Hidden Worlders don't like him, and even ghosts don't like his company much. Now, under your feet is a trapdoor which leads to a tunnel that will take you to one of the shuttle stations. Catch a car and tell it to take you to Doctor Noname. Then he's to take you to the Guardian. You can't get there on the shuttle. Once you're back in Owlchurch, go straight to London, and don't delay. Don't look back, don't think of me, just go, OK?'

'Yes, Mum,' said Thomas, sadly.

Pinch stared at him. 'What's up?'

Thomas told him.

'Then she must fear it's you who he . . .'

Pinch broke off, but Thomas didn't notice. After taking a last look at his mother, standing talking with Mister D, he found the trapdoor and went down into the darkness beyond, with Pinch following close behind him.

They raced down the tunnel below and at its end came to a shuttle station. It was smaller than the one near Doctor Noname's. They jumped into one of the carriages and ordered it to take them at full speed to Doctor Noname's. *Twang, twang!* The silver wires broke and the carriage hurtled away, making Thomas's teeth rattle. It sped back over the island, going rather faster than before, so all they could see was a blur beneath them. Very soon, the carriage stopped in mid-air, and tumbled the boys down, down, down, then swung away again and vanished.

Picking themselves up, a little bruised and shaken, they saw they were in the white passageway outside Doctor Noname's room. They raced down it and pounded on the door at the end.

'Who's there?' quavered Doctor Noname's voice.

'It's me, Thomas! And Pinch! Mum said you have to take us to the Guardian straight away!

Mister D's at her place! She's trying to slow him down! Our bracelets are withering! Quick!'

The door suddenly opened. Doctor Noname stood there. 'Oh, dear, oh dear,' he declared. The blue eyes behind the mask blinked unhappily. 'Better get you to the Guardian, then . . .'

'Am I glad to find someone in this dump apart from my annoying niece!' said Alice's uncle, grinning at Patch. 'You're going to help me, little thing.'

No I'm not, Patch wanted to yell, but found she couldn't say anything at all. Her tongue seemed to be frozen. She glared at the man, who grinned even more broadly.

'Dagger looks won't help, child.' He looked around and pointed at a corner of the room. 'Go and bring me that chest over there. It'll do to put this brat in.'

I won't, I won't, thought Patch, furiously, but she couldn't help it. Her feet dragged her to the chest, her hands pulled the chest over to Alice's uncle without her being able to do anything about it.

The man was obviously enjoying himself hugely. 'Better and better,' he said, 'this spell really does work well here! I knew I was good and only needed the chance to show it in the right environment.'

He gestured at Patch to open the chest. She did it, without wanting to. Alice's uncle tumbled the girl into the chest and, before she could spring up, he'd slammed the lid down on her and slid the bolt across. 'There, that'll keep her quiet for a while. Or rather,' he added, raising an eyebrow as Alice's furious kicks and yells could be heard coming from within the chest, 'it'll keep her out of action for a bit. Now you, little thing – what's your name, by the way?'

I won't tell you, thought Patch. But she opened her mouth and found herself saying, 'Patch Gull.'

'And now, Patch Gull,' said Alice's uncle, beaming, 'you're going to take me to your leader. I'm here to fill the vacancy, see. Yes, sir, James Grimm's their man, and my requirements are very reasonable, you'll find.'

Patch stared at him. What on earth was he talking about? Was the man mad?

'You're in awe of me, aren't you, fairy child? Funny, I always thought fairies were supposed to be pretty, but you're only *pretty ugly*, seems to me.' He laughed at his own bad joke. 'Anyway, don't let's dilly-dally.'

Patch made a huge effort at freeing herself from the spell. She could feel it tightening around her like elastic, but if she pushed hard at one side, she might make it snap. She pushed, and pushed, and managed to break the hold a little, enough to take a couple of steps back, and then turn and run for the stairs. But she never made it. A hand shot out and gripped her ankle, painfully, and she fell over. Blue eyes that had suddenly turned icy burned into her own. 'Not so fast, little thing,' said James Grimm, viciously. 'Not so fast, you . . .' He broke off. 'Well, well, and what do we have here?'

'No! No!' shouted Patch, but she was powerless to move as the wizard tightened the spell around her again and bent down to the floor. She could only stare in terrified horror as he reached for the things that had flown out of her pocket when she fell. The dolls!

James Grimm picked them up. He looked at Patch. 'Hmm,' he said. 'Important to you, eh?' He made as if to squash them between his hands.

A raw yell burst out of Patch. 'No!'

'I see,' said James Grimm. He frowned, turning the dolls over in his hands. 'What are you up to, eh, I wonder, little thing? Never mind,' he went on, pocketing the dolls, 'you'll do what I say now, I bet. If you don't do just as I say, my dear, these little puppets of yours, I'll grind them to pieces under my heel, or set fire to them, or drown them.' He smiled at Patch's horrified face. 'Yes, yes, I see I'm right. Don't worry, my dear, I don't take dolls from little girls unless they've been very, very naughty, and I'm sure you won't be, will you? You'll help me, won't you?'

Patch glared at him. But she nodded, hopelessly.

'OK. Then do what I asked. Lead on, kid.'

I could wait for Father, thought Patch in sudden hope. He'll deal with this upstart Obbo. But James Grimm was watching her face. He said, patting his pocket, 'And no tricks either, little thing, or – squash, crush – your dolls will bite the dust. Get it? Now, my friends told me to head for Owlchurch. Know it?'

Compelled by the spell, Patch nodded. But she was puzzled. Who were these friends? The ones Alice had seen? Clearly, they must have come to the Hidden World themselves at some stage. Maybe they'd been one of the guests at the recent Magicians' Convention. But why had they helped him? And what did James Grimm actually want? What was this 'vacancy' he referred to? She had a really bad feeling about it all. This man was trouble, serious trouble, and not only for her and her friends. He was exactly the sort you didn't want in the Hidden World. There was something greedy, grasping and frantic about him.

She must leave a warning for her father, or Skrob when he got back, she thought. Not only to warn them, but also to let them know of Alice's plight.

The girl was still kicking and yelling, but the sounds were getting fainter. Now Patch heard a sob. Then another. Poor Alice, thought Patch. But what can I do to help her? I'm helpless myself. Silly girl, she thought, then, crossly. She'd said her uncle was no good as a wizard. That was obviously untrue. He was very, very good. The holding spell was very strong.

'After you,' said James Grimm, gesturing up the stairs. Patch obeyed, but as she went up, she brushed against the wall. Quick as thought, she sent a tiny spell down her arm, where it buried itself in the wall. It was the last bit of magic energy she had left. The tiny spell, which acted as an alarm, would flash the moment someone came in, and alert them that something bad had happened.

She shot a look back at James Grimm. He hadn't noticed anything. Come what may, Patch thought, I must get those dolls back from him, or Thomas and Pinch will be doomed.

'Now which one's the right one today?' In the passage outside his room, Doctor Noname was staring at the pictures on the wall.

They weren't misty any more. Thomas could see the landscape in each picture now. One was of a wild heath where the wind blew; another of a tall, snowy mountain-top;

and another one of a cave by the side of a stormy sea. As he looked, suddenly he thought he saw a figure, cloaked all in white, appear at the mouth of the cave – or was that on the mountain – or there, flitting across the heath?

'This one, I think,' said Doctor Noname, and he touched the painting of the cave by the sea. Immediately, it grew enormous, blowing up like a giant balloon, engulfing the three of them. And now they were standing on the rocky shores of a sea getting stormier by the second. Thunder cracked, lightning flashed, the sky grew dark and the wind howled. The waves rose higher and higher.

'Hang on to me!' came Doctor Noname's voice, faint in the gathering storm. 'Hang on to me, and don't let go!'

So they clung on with all their might to the tall, thin ghost who, though he bent like a reed under the gale, plunged bravely on across the shore towards the cave, gaping blackly like a toothless mouth at them.

A wave rose higher than the others and washed over them. As it did, Thomas suddenly heard screams and groans and rending sounds; and saw, in the heart of the wave, a tall sailing ship breaking up before his very eyes. He saw sailors clinging desperately to bits of wreckage, with the sea roaring around them; and he saw, coming up from below, a frightful procession: a silent grey ship, shark-shaped, with a black flag flying from its mast, rising up from the depths, and behind and in front of it, four huge fish with razor-sharp teeth. One was red, one grey, one yellow, one black; and on their backs were creatures of nightmare, with skull-faces and empty eye sockets. Silently, they moved up, past him, and the Riders plucked the sailors straight off the wreckage they were clinging on to, and dived down with them, down, down, into the depths of the ocean. Then the wave fell back and away, and Thomas saw that he was quite dry, and not wet at all, as you might have thought. But he was trembling so hard that he would have lost his grip on Doctor Noname, if the old ghost hadn't seized hold of his wrist and gripped it tight.

'Nearly there! Nearly there!' he called, his voice a whisper above the noise.

Now they were battling against the wind, which seemed to push them one step back each time they took two steps forward. Then a big grey cloud rushed at them, and Thomas could see faces in that, too; staring faces with blood-red eyes and cruel lips and bony hands stretched out for him. His heart filled with dread and his teeth chattered with cold. Then he closed his eyes and thought of his mother in her beautiful meadow full of flowers, and suddenly, it was as if sunlight was washing through him again.

He opened his eyes. The wind had died down, the grey cloud rolled away. He looked over at Pinch – and yelled.

'Doctor Noname! It's Pinch! He's started to disappear!'

Pinch's left arm, where the browning bracelet hung, was fading away ... Pinch couldn't speak; but his eyes, terrified, helpless, rolled madly in his face.

'Hang on! Hang on!' shouted Doctor Noname. 'We're almost there!'

They were just about at the cave mouth now. In another instant they would be plunging into the darkness beyond ...

'I wonder,' said James Grimm, as they walked through the Green Man's rooms, 'I wonder why you are so keen on these toys?'

Patch felt sick. The wizard had taken the dolls out of his pockets and was looking at them, curiously. He rubbed at the figure that was Pinch, rubbed at its arm, fiddled with the bracelet – which, to her horror, Patch saw was fast turning brown. 'Funny little creature – looks rather like you. Is it meant to be you, I wonder?'

'Please,' Patch managed to force herself to whisper, 'I'll do anything you want. Please — just leave them alone.'

James Grimm looked at her, then at the dolls again. There was a little frown on his face. 'Now I *am* interested.' He put the dolls back in his pocket. 'I think you'll have to tell me what these are, little thing, before we're through.'

Patch said nothing. She was trying very hard to gather enough energy for a bit of magic. But the man was too strong for her. She couldn't even conjure up a bit of minor glamour.

She came to the entrance of the tree and touched the bark. The tree swung open and they stepped through into the wood beyond. Behind them, the entrance closed again, smoothly. The wizard's eyebrows lifted. 'Very neat,' he murmured. 'Now I wonder whether that's the kind of house I'll ask for? Or something grander, perhaps? What do you think, little Patch?'

Patch didn't know what he was talking

about. Did this . . . this crook, this creature, think people were going to welcome him, give him a house? Was he mad? No wizard would ever be allowed to live in the Hidden World, and certainly not a wicked one like this. The thought gave her courage. Once they got to Owlchurch, the others could help. It didn't matter any more about telling them where Pinch and Thomas were. All of them together could overpower James Grimm. She could rescue the dolls and race down to the river . . .

She looked up at the sky. Was it getting darker? It might well be late afternoon, now. Not very long till sunset . . . not long till sunset . . . She felt suddenly very, very scared. What if they didn't get back in time? What if she couldn't get the dolls back? She must, she *must*, think of something to get away from him.

TWELVE

There was a stink coming from the mouth of the cave. A terrible stink, which filled Thomas's nose and head. But it was the least of his worries. He kept an anxious eye on Pinch, but after that terrible moment, the Hidden Worlder seemed to have recovered. But it must be a warning they were getting very close to the time when Pinch could no longer stand the air of the Island of Ghosts.

He tried to speak, to call across to Pinch, but his voice had stopped in his throat. He could feel an odd ache in his shadow limbs. But he had no time to think of it, for in the next moment, they were in the cave, and the stink was all around them. Pinch's nose wrinkled, too; but Doctor Noname did not even seem to notice. He plunged on into the thick smelly darkness, holding the boys tightly by the hand.

'Guardian!' he called. 'The living must go back, before it's too late!'

But nobody answered. Nothing happened, and still Doctor Noname kept calling.

Patch and Grimm hurried through the woods. They would soon be at Patch's own cottage, and still no idea had come to her. Grimm left the dolls in his pocket now, but Patch had an uneasy feeling that he wouldn't do so for long. She was terribly worried. As the trees thinned out, she could see that the sky was filling with pink and orange cloud as the sun slid slowly down.

There was her house. The door was open. Mother must be in. Patch felt a little sick. Mother might be able to help, but she must be furious already at what the three children had done. And now there was Grimm . . . How could she get rid of him? Who could help her?

Suddenly, it came to her. She turned away from the house and went down the hill, heading for the village. She hoped Mother wouldn't see her out of the window.

At least she had an advantage over Grimm. He was a stranger and didn't know who was the leader here. Now, she thought, let's hope there's nobody hanging about.

She was lucky. The village seemed deserted, though she could see signs of activity around the Apple Tree Café. Maybe they were all in there . . . Oh no, she thought. Please, let the one I'm looking for not be there, or I've had it.

She took the track that led to the back of the village shops. Grimm sauntered after her, quite unconcerned. Ah, another piece of luck. The back door of the place she wanted was ajar. She beckoned to Grimm. He smiled, pleased with himself. He patted his pocket. 'Remember, any tricks, my dear, and it's curtains for this little lot.'

Patch swallowed. What she was about to do was very dangerous. But she couldn't think of anything else. There was no one else she could turn to.

Deeper they went into the cave and it got even darker. So dark that Thomas could soon see nothing at all. Still Doctor Noname kept calling, and then, just as Thomas thought no one would ever answer, a voice came.

'You are too late. I cannot help you.'

'No,' said Doctor Noname, 'no, Guardian, you must help them across.'

'It's too late,' said the voice. 'I can do nothing for them.'

'Then I will help them,' said Doctor Noname.

'You cannot. Or you might be trapped between the worlds. Then not only will you not know your name, but you will even lose what you love here, your room, your studies, everything.'

'But I said I'd help them. Their mother asked me to take them,' said Doctor Noname, and Thomas could feel the old ghost's hand quivering in his. 'I must do this, or they will die.'

But the Guardian did not answer and the cave was quiet again. The darkness pressed like a suffocating blanket around them and the stink grew stronger. Then, suddenly, they heard another noise: a kind of low, growling sound, that slowly grew into a dull roaring. Mister D and his Riders were very close!

Patch and Grimm went into the shop. It was dim and close, and the figure crouching by something on the floor was difficult to see properly. But Patch thought she recognised the cap, the coat. She ran forward, and tapped the figure on the shoulder.

It jumped – and turned around, snarling. And to her horror, Patch saw not the face she'd been hoping for, but one she hated. And she

also saw what it had been crouching over . . .
She tried to back away, but Grimm got hold of
her and dragged her forward. He was smiling.

'Why, hello, my friend,' he said, brightly.
'Welcoming committee?'

The creature grinned, showing pointed
teeth. 'You could say we thought you might
need our help,' it said, in an unpleasant,
squeaky voice. It looked at Patch. 'Long time
no see,' it growled, deep in its throat. 'Bet you
thought I could never get away, didn't you?
Well, you see, things are changing, once again,
at home. We've got a chance, now. A grand
alliance – a historic opportunity, you might
say, and even our stick-in-the-mud Queen will
have to see that.' It turned back to Grimm.
'The girl brought you here because this
thing . . .' and he kicked contemptuously at the
unconscious heap on the floor that was
Hinkypunk, the Owlchurch Trickster, 'this
thing was the only one here who might be able
to break through the spells we gave you. That's

because he's got more than a touch of Nightmare in him, the dirty traitor. Well, I've dealt with him for the time being, and the others are being dealt with. They'll soon be eating out of your hand, Grimm my dear.'

'Excellent,' said Grimm. He looked at Patch and smiled, nastily. 'So, despite what I told you, you tried to trick me, eh?' He put his hand in his pocket.

'No, please, please!' The words burst from Patch. 'Please, don't . . .'

'Ah-ha,' said the creature, craning its head – something like a monkey's, something like a tortoise's – to look at what Grimm was pulling out of his pocket. 'What do we have here?'

'Her dolls,' said Grimm. 'She seems to love them well enough.'

Fustian Jargon – for it was indeed the nasty secretary of the Uncouther royal family – laughed, harshly. 'You fool,' it said. 'Don't you know anything? They are guarantees of safety for two living beings to cross into the world of ghosts.' He peered at the bracelet. 'And it looks to me like they'd better get back fast, or they'll get stuck there.'

'Well, so what?' said Grimm, sulkily. Clearly, he did not enjoy being called a fool.

'So what? Ask her who they are, you fool. Ask her!'

'No,' said Patch, 'no, I won't.' But suddenly, she felt a terrible pain as they made the spell tighten around her, hard, cutting into her so that she thought she might stop breathing.

'Tell me, little thing,' said Grimm, 'or I destroy them anyway, no matter what.'

'They're . . . they're my friends.' The words tore through Patch. 'My friend – and my brother.'

'Ah, but what friend?' said Fustian Jargon, his hands like claws reaching up to her, his wicked eyes glittering. 'Tell him, Patch Gull. Tell him.'

Patch fought the words. She fought them so hard that she thought she would faint from the pain of it.

And she managed to hold them back.

'Tell me,' screeched Grimm, his hand hovering over the dolls. 'Tell me, or it's all over.'

Patch struggled. And still she managed to stay quiet.

But Fustian Jargon shrugged. 'What matter? I can tell you. It's the Rymer. It's Thomas Trew.'

'The Rymer!' said Grimm, sounding bewildered. 'But I thought . . . I thought . . . You told me . . .'

'I told you there was a vacancy,' said Fustian Jargon, smoothly. 'And so there will be, and very soon.' In one swift movement, he grabbed the dolls from Grimm. He grinned at Patch. 'You poor fools. Never dreamed you'd make it so easy for us,' and then, as poor, spellbound Patch watched, frozen with horror, pain and despair, he methodically destroyed the dolls, pulling them to pieces with great thoroughness, stamping on the pieces. Then he said a few words and, all at once, tongues of fire appeared on the pieces, licking up leaves, straw, sticks, the grass bracelet, and then the sock, the scrap from Pinch's shirt, even the little pebbles Patch had used for eyes seeming to melt in the heat.

'That'll cook their goose well and truly,' said Fustian Jargon, with great satisfaction. He smiled at Patch. 'Thomas should not have offended and hurt and baffled and bamboozled so many of us,' he said. 'Everywhere he went, he made enemies, who ended up with a common cause – his defeat. And now our revenge has come, and won't it be sweet! Things are going to change around here, my dear Patch Gull, now that the old Rymer is no more and we can install a new one. Oh yes, James Grimm will be our new Rymer. He's a very talented man, and a clever one. He sees things our way. Things are going to be very, very different indeed in this world. You'd better get used to it.'

'Fustian, my friend,' said Grimm, fretfully, 'let's forget about her. She's a little thing of no account. How about me? I want to be crowned Rymer, or whatever you do, and very soon.'

'Of course you do, dear chap,' said Fustian, soothingly, 'and we're going to go and organise that very soon. Better go and see how Astrolir's getting on, eh?'

Astrolir, thought Patch, I recognise that name too. The wicked Ariel who had put that horrid spell on Thomas that nearly killed him. It really was an alliance of villains and crooks.

Fustian Jargon was still talking. 'First of all, best put these two out of action for a bit longer.' He made a couple of gestures in the air and at once from his fingers grew a kind of tangle of fine, sticky thread, which fell on Patch, rolling her up as tightly as a fly in a spider's web. More of the same on Hinkypunk, and now the two of them were helplessly bound, unable to move. But Patch hardly cared. All she could think about was that she would never see Pinch or Thomas alive again and, beside that, nothing that might happen to her, or to the Hidden World under the dictatorship of the wicked creatures, seemed to matter at all . . .

A terrible pain was shooting through Thomas. But his mind was calm. He saw that the grass bracelet around his wrist had turned quite black. He thought, I'm going to die . . . no, I am actually dying. It really is too late . . . too late . . .

'You can't,' said Doctor Noname's voice, very close to his ear. 'No, I won't let you. I won't!'

Oh, you're hurting me, Thomas wanted to scream, as he felt the power of the ghost's hold. Let me go, let me go. Mister D has come to get me, and that's OK, I don't mind . . . Mum's on the island, and she'll be happy to see me, and I . . .

'No, you can't,' cried the ghost. 'What of your friend? What of Pinch? He can't be a ghost. He will just blow away and vanish. He'll be nothing, nothing, do you hear! Hold on to me, hold tight! I'm going to try and make a bridge with the Hidden World . . .'

The words seemed to come to Thomas from a great distance but, as they fell on his dying ears, they roused an unease that grew and grew. Pinch, he thought. Pinch. He'll be nothing. Nothing . . . I can't let that happen . . . Can't . . . But it's so hard. It hurts, to hold on, when to let go is so much better, gentler, sweeter; to let go, to float here in the space between life and death, waiting for Mister D to take him . . .

All at once, there was Mister D. The lord of death had the window of his car wound down and he was staring at Thomas through his sightless eyes. Thomas saw the thin lips move, but he could not quite make out what he said. He thought Mister D must be calling him to take that last ride with him, and so he moved forward. But Mister D shook his head, wound up the window, and tapped sharply on it. The Riders revved up their motorbikes and, in an instant, Mister D's car and its escort vanished from sight. And Thomas was left floating, no longer in death or in life but in a kind of in-between world of shadow and fog and mist where he no longer knew a thing.

'Patch,' said Hinkypunk's voice suddenly, sounding a little cracked but still very much his voice. 'Patch, don't take on so. It's not the end, you know. Not yet.'

'But they're gone,' said Patch dully, finding she could talk freely now, but no longer caring. 'The dolls are destroyed and now they can never get back.'

'Nonsense,' said Hinkypunk. 'The ways of the Ghost World aren't as simple as all that, you know.'

'But the Guardian said they couldn't get back if the dolls were lost and the bracelet withered,' said Patch. 'And the Guardian would know.'

'He may not have told you everything,

you know,' said Hinkypunk, and his voice sounded more jaunty by the second. 'Don't you know, Guardians are like the Tricksters of the Ghost World?'

'So what?' said Patch, but now a tiny bit of hope was stirring in her.

'Well, takes one to know one,' said Hinkypunk, brightly. 'I might be able to work out how his mind works, though I could do with some help, I must say. Hey, that's right,' he went on, 'I remember now. There's a book in Monotype's bookshop, it's all about the Ghost World, quite an authority, I do believe. We might be able to get a clue from that.'

Patch gulped, suddenly remembering the book in question disappearing down a hole in the river bank. In a small voice, she said, 'But we're tied up. We can't get out of here . . .'

'We need to get a message to Monotype,' said Hinkypunk. 'Well, I might be tied up, so I can't use my limbs, but I can still use my voice.' And he whistled, long and low and clear.

There was a stirring behind Patch and something flapped past her. Hinkypunk whistled again, in several different pitches. Patch knew that was how he talked to some of his tricksy things. She couldn't see properly, because of the spider's web clustered thickly around her face, but she could hear the scratching of little claws and the hissing of a little voice. Hinkypunk's whistling stopped, and then he said, 'OK, Patch. The gadfly's gone, and won't stop pestering Monotype till he listens to it. We'll have the book here in a jiffy and then we'll find the right thing to do to bring them back.'

Inside Patch, the tiny hope faded again. The book . . . the book's gone, she thought. It's escaped, run away, and they'll never find it . . .

'Hinkypunk,' she said, bravely, 'there's something I have to tell you.'

Something was pulling him down, down, down. Thomas didn't even try to struggle any more. He just let the thing, whatever it was, pull him down through layers and layers of fog and mist and shadow, through coldness that would have turned his blood to ice, if it had been flowing normally in his veins, and then through heat so fierce that his skin would have fried off his bones if he hadn't been shadow and mist himself. Still, he was pulled, down, down, and now his mind was beginning to work again, his heart gave a stutter and started to beat again. His toes started to tingle, painfully, his ears to buzz with sound. Cloud rushed past his face, thick at first, but very soon thinning, and a breeze blew against his face, and then he felt something warm seeping into him, sunlight maybe, or just life. He could feel it rushing into him as he fell the last little while, through cloudless blue sky, and then, whizzing past trees, and then *bump!* on the ground, bouncing once or twice then coming to a rest.

His eyes opened. There were tall trees above

him, and one of those trees bent down to him and spoke to him. 'It's good to see you, lad.'

Thomas didn't know where he was at first, and thought he must have imagined the tree speaking to him; then his heart gave a big thud, back into its proper place, his muddled thoughts cleared, and he whispered, 'Oh, it's you, Green Man.' Behind the Green Man, he could see the edge of the wood and Old Gal's cottage, and then he remembered what had happened and sat up too suddenly, crying, 'Pinch! Pinch! Oh, no, where's Pinch?'

'My son is safe and sound,' said the Green Man, gently. 'Sleeping. Exhausted, but safe. His mother's with him.'

His head spinning, Thomas fell back. 'How did it . . . how did we . . . I don't understand . . .'

'You were both saved by the sacrifice of a great heart,' said the Green Man. 'He paid a terrible price, making himself the bridge for you to get back, for his spirit was wrenched away from the island, and he is fated to wander the space between the worlds now, lost and homeless for ever.'

'Doctor Noname,' cried Thomas. 'Oh, poor Doctor Noname. It was what he was most afraid of. Oh, Green Man, I had promised to find out his name, but didn't, because I was too scared of Mister D. He helped us so much, and now I cannot even repay him . . .'

'There are some things that must be borne,' said the Green Man, and he helped Thomas to his feet and walked him to the door of the cottage. 'You must go in to the others and rest,' he said, 'and not come out till I come to tell you. For there is great danger for you down in the village, and much work to do to get rid of it.'

'Patch . . .' began Thomas, but the Green Man pushed him in the cottage and closed and locked the door, saying, 'You go in and see them and wait. It will be all right, you'll see.'

Thomas went in. There, in the twins' bedroom, was Pinch, looking pale, bruised and very shaken, lying in his bed. By his side sat his mother, and on a chair facing them, a complete stranger – a girl a little younger than Thomas, with fair plaits and brown eyes and a rather dirty face. 'Oh, hello,' she said. 'You must be Thomas the Rymer.'

Thomas looked at her, baffled. 'Who are you?' he said. 'And where's Patch?'

'Never mind, child,' said Hinkypunk. 'That second gadfly I sent will bring someone to our rescue. And once we're freed, we'll look for the book. It can't have got far. I've got tricks I can send down that hole in the river bank to sting it so bad it will come rushing back. Never you fret, child.'

But Patch did fret. What if the hole led to a tunnel? What if the book fell through into the Uncouthers' country? But at least thinking about that stopped her from thinking about the likely fate of her brother and her best friend. She couldn't see the sky, trussed up like she was, but it must be past sunset now. Oh, she'd give anything to turn the clock back, she thought. Anything to be back this morning, before they'd made their fateful decision to go to the island . . .

The door crashed open. A familiar voice shouted, 'By the horns of Pan! What's been happening here!'

'Father!' yelled Patch. 'Father, it's me! And Hinkypunk! We're tied up!'

'So you are,' said the Green Man calmly, and the next thing Patch knew, she was being lifted up in the knotty arms of her father and his twiggy claws were working delicately, carefully, to remove the sticky web from Patch's body. At last, he worked it loose, and Patch was free.

'Oh, Father!' she said, and looked into his deep, sad eyes. 'Father – Pinch . . . he's . . .'

'Alive and well,' said her father, brightly, 'at least, he will be well. And so is your friend, Thomas. They're at home,' he went on, as

Patch jumped down from his arms, 'and you run there just as fast as you can and stay there with them and lock the door, because there's a great fight coming and I don't want any of you children to be near it.'

And so saying, he turned his attention to Hinkypunk, while Patch took to her heels just as fast as she could, heading for her own cottage at the top of the hill.

But she never quite made it, for just as she was running up the path to the door, someone stepped out from the bushes at the side of the path.

'And just where are you going so fast, little thing?' said James Grimm. 'Going to introduce me to your friends, are you?' Quick as lightning, he grabbed at her, and with one hand held her in a tight grip. Something flashed in his other hand and, to her horror, Patch saw it was a knife – but not just any knife. With its wicked, misshapen blade, it looked like an Uncouther thing, forged in the fires of Nightmare. Yet the spell engraved on it wasn't Uncouther; for it was written in a script only the Ariels used. The smell about it was a rotting sea-smell; and the carved handle of the knife was of a shining gold only found in Montaynard mines. And surely, surely the design had more than a hint of Middler artistry about it. It was a weapon such as she'd never seen before.

Grimm saw her expression. 'A new thing my friends just brought for me,' he said, happily. 'It combines all the dark forces of this world. They say that just one nick from this will poison anyone's blood. Lovely, isn't it?'

Patch glared at him, but he only smiled. 'Sorry you don't agree. But no matter. In we go, little thing. Can't miss the reunion, now can we?'

THIRTEEN

I'm sorry,' Patch kept repeating a few seconds later, 'I'm sorry. I couldn't stop him.'

'Oh, do zip that mouth of yours,' said James Grimm, 'You're beginning to seriously bore me, and that's a mistake, let me tell you. No, don't move, dear lady,' he went on, gesturing to Old Gal, 'or this ugly little kid of yours will get the knife across her throat. Don't tell me it won't hurt her. I know what it can do. I've been told. It invades the blood; won't kill one of you lot, unlike humans, but it will twist and deform you and make you hopeless and mindless exiles from your own world. I'm not afraid to use it, oh, not one little bit. Now then, little thing,

166

introduce me to your friends and relatives. Come on, I don't want to have to ask twice.'

'My brother, Pi . . . Pinch,' said Patch, brokenly, pointing at the bed. 'My mother, Old Gal. And . . . and my friend, Thomas Trew.'

'Ah, yes, the old Rymer. And his new friend, I see, my not-very-dear niece.'

'Uncle Jim,' said Alice, desperately, 'please, there's no need to be horrid and wave knives around. I'm sure that whatever you want, if you ask nicely, people will let you have it.'

James Grimm laughed. 'You always were a sentimental fool. Just like your stupid father, my unlamented late brother. Now then, boy,' he went on, turning to Thomas, 'before you have to leave us, tell me – do you have any tips for the new Rymer?'

Thomas stared at him. 'You! Are you really a Rymer?'

'My friends tell me I am. They say I'm to be the greatest ever, to rule over everything.'

'That's silly. Being a Rymer isn't the same as

being a king or an emperor or anything like that,' said Thomas.

James Grimm sneered, 'You know nothing. A Rymer can control so much, if he chooses to. If he really has the gifts necessary and the boldness, he can make the whole world dance to his tune. He can force the whole world to 'live in his stories and his pictures and his spells. Nobody else will ever be able to create anything else. He will become the Rymer of all Rymers, and he is the one who will control all dreams, all imagination, everything.' He paused a moment, then preening himself, added, 'And that's me, of course. I'm multi-talented, brilliant, the greatest creative mind who ever lived. I had ancestors who were storytellers – you may have heard of them, the Brothers Grimm – but they are peas, ants, grains of dust, compared to me. I am the greatest. I am the Rymer to end all Rymers. And I will rule over the Hidden World for ever.'

'You're mad,' said Thomas. 'No one can do that. It doesn't work like that!'

'Are you quite sure?' said a new voice, and Fustian Jargon stepped into the room. There was someone else behind him – someone else Thomas had hoped he'd never, ever see again. He took a step back. Fustian was grinning. 'Ah, dear Thomas, I see you are surprised to see me again. Thought the Queen had grounded me for ever, didn't you? Well, as it happens, I've regained my old position at Court now, and the General's power is rising again. You see, he and I are still angry with what you did, and we wanted to punish you, but until dear Astrolir here came to us with a good plan, we weren't sure how to go about it.'

'Good day to you, Thomas,' said Astrolir, stepping out from behind Fustian. 'A gathering of old friends, I see.'

Thomas couldn't help shivering as he looked at the wicked Ariel's deceptively gentle face and remembered his own despair, trapped in Astrolir's spell, up in the sky.

'Yes,' said Fustian, looking from one to the other, his tongue licking his lips, 'Astrolir thought the best way to deal with you and your meddling was to get rid of you and find ourselves a new Rymer – our own candidate. And so we enlisted the help of others you've wronged – like Cirsea the Syren and her servants, and Ralf Ravenbeard and his trolls, and many others who hate you and what you've done. We scoured the world for a suitable Rymer. And we found one. The perfect one.'

'You see?' said James Grimm, preening himself. 'That's me they're talking about.'

Thomas ignored him. He looked at Fustian and Astrolir. 'You won't get away with it! The others will stop you! You can't impose this man on them!'

Fustian laughed. 'The forces of darkness are very strong right now. Once we have the new Rymer installed, we will take over everything, through him. There's an invasion party being readied as we speak. Then, when we control the Hidden World, we'll take over the Obvious World as well! And there's nothing anyone of your friends in the Hidden World can do about it.'

Astrolir eyed Alice. 'And no human can, either. So don't even think about it. One good twist from that lovely knife our dear Grimm is holding, dear little girl, and you will go mad. Stark, staring mad, as the worst nightmares in all the worlds assail you and torment you without rest. Another little twist, and you're dead. Deadibones, my dear.'

'You're overlooking one thing,' said Thomas.

'What's that?' sniffed Fustian.

'Me,' said Thomas, trying not to tremble.

Astrolir laughed. 'You! You're going to be no trouble to us, very soon. We know the poison of the Huntsman's arrow is still in you. We know the island appeared here to warn you. You could have escaped your fate by going back to your own world. But like a fool, you chose not to. So Mister D is on his way to you, sure as sure.'

'Who's Mister D?' said Grimm, sharply.

'The lord of death,' said Fustian, impatiently.

'But he's not after me,' said Thomas.

'Nonsense. How would you know?' snapped Astrolir.

'Because he spoke to me,' said Thomas. In his mind, he could see again, suddenly, the picture: Mister D and his Riders, sweeping through the sky; and the window wound down, the sightless eyes staring, the thin lips opening to say something. Suddenly, he could see the exact shape of that something. 'He said it wasn't my time.'

Fustian stared at him. For the first time, he looked uncertain. 'Nonsense,' he repeated. 'No one meets Mister D and escapes. Isn't that right, Astrolir?'

The Ariel blinked. 'I . . . I'm sure that's right.'

'You know it's not,' said Old Gal, speaking

for the first time. 'There is one way to escape. If he takes someone else instead.' She scowled at Grimm. 'You, I think you told us, are a Rymer. And it's a Rymer he's after.'

'What?' In his agitation, Grimm dropped Patch, who lost no time in scurrying to her mother's side. Grimm took no notice. He rounded on Fustian. 'Is this true?'

But it was Thomas who answered. 'It is definitely a Rymer he's after. The island only appears if a Rymer is in mortal danger. If there's more than one Rymer – and if you're a Rymer, then it's you and me, Mr Grimm – then that means he's after one or the other of us. And as he told me it wasn't my time, well, it must be *yours*.'

'Shut up, you!' yelled Grimm. Knife held in front of him, he advanced menacingly on Fustian and Astrolir. 'Why didn't you tell me this? You said it was that boy who was going to die!'

The Ariel and the Uncouther smiled

soothingly. 'Now, now, don't get agitated, dear boy,' said Astrolir, stepping back. 'We knew it was a Rymer Mister D's after. And it must be the boy. He's lying. He can't have spoken to Mister D.'

'Yes, yes, he's playing for time,' said Fustian Jargon, 'just playing for time.'

'Time I don't have, if that's true,' said Thomas. 'Mister D will be here very soon. If I'm not telling the truth about what he said, why am I just staying here?'

Fustian glared at him. 'You are trying to trick us,' he declared.

'Am I? Do you really think I want to die?'

Astrolir yelled, 'You are a liar, a thief, a crook, a wicked creature!'

'My, my, how honest you are describing yourselves,' snapped Old Gal. 'But if you know what's good for you, you two and your false Rymer will take yourselves off mighty smart before Mister D turns up. Which will be, as Thomas says, very soon.'

'You witch! Who are you calling a false Rymer?' screeched James Grimm. 'I'm going to make sure Mister D takes the one he should!' And, quick as a flash, he threw the knife straight at Thomas. But as he did so, Alice darted forward in front of him, and so it was the girl who was hit. Because she was a little shorter than Thomas, though, it didn't hit her in the heart, as it would have done Thomas, but glanced off her shoulder, drawing blood. Instantly, she fell like a stone, without a sound.

'Alice!' cried Patch, running to her. In the same moment, from outside came the sound of a low growl, louder and louder.

'It's him! It's Mister D! Run!' yelled Fustian at Grimm and Astrolir.

'Stop them!' shouted Old Gal, but it was too late. Forgetting the knife and everything else, Fustian, Astrolir and James Grimm had taken to their heels and fled as fast as they could possibly go, and no one could catch them up, even if they'd wanted to. But they didn't. All their attention was on poor Alice, whose colour was rapidly going from pink to grey.

'Quick,' said Old Gal to Pinch and Patch, 'get me the healing ointments and herbs. Thomas, a basin of warm water . . . Quick, or Mister D might pick up another passenger.'

They hurried to get everything she'd asked. Outside, the growling sound was getting steadily, relentlessly, louder and louder. Racing back with the warm water, Thomas said, 'When we were on the island, we hid from Mister D in Mum's house. She said that her love hid me from his sight. Can't we do that here, Mrs Gull? Can't we?'

'I don't know,' said Old Gal, rubbing ointment on Alice's face and arms. 'Maybe it only worked on the island. And your mother loved you so much. We hardly know this girl. And she's the niece of that man, what's more.'

'Yes, but she saved my life,' said Thomas, softly.

Patch said, 'And she's a good sort. She really is . . .'

'Well, let's try,' said Old Gal. 'Hold hands, everyone, form a circle around her. Let me do the talking. And don't drop your hands, whatever you do! Quick!'

FOURTEEN

The car and its escort had drawn up outside the cottage. The door was flung open. Mister D stood in the doorway, flanked by two of his Riders.

'Good evening,' said Mister D. This time, Thomas heard him plainly. It was a soft, pleasant voice, without emotion of any sort. Yet it sent cold shivers down Thomas's back. 'I believe I have a passenger to pick up here,' Mister D went on.

'I'm sorry, sir,' said Old Gal. 'I think you are mistaken.'

Mister D shook his head. 'There is no mistake. The Rymer must come with me.'

'Rymer?' said Old Gal, sharply. The twins

threw an anguished glance at Thomas, who began to shake like a leaf. Was it him who had made the mistake? Had he imagined Mister D's words, earlier? He would have dropped the others' hands if they hadn't been gripping his so tightly.

'You can't have Thomas,' said Old Gal, firmly, though her eyes were bleak. 'We won't let you. He's our own Rymer.'

'He's our friend,' burst out Pinch.

'And we love him,' said Patch, defiantly.

'There's nothing for you here,' said Old Gal. 'Nothing, Mister D.'

'Who said anything about a Thomas?' said Mister D, with a hint of impatience. 'If you mean the boy, I've already told him. It's not his time.'

'If you're looking for that other Rymer, James Grimm—' began Old Gal, but Mister D interrupted her, with a cross wave of his hand.

'Not James Grimm. It is *Alice* Grimm I have come for,' he said.

'What? Then . . .'

'Didn't you know? She's a Rymer. Not even properly aware of it, yet, but she could have been a good one, if she'd lived.'

'But we . . . we didn't realise . . .'

'Neither did she,' said Mister D, sharply.

Thomas spoke for the first time. An idea had come to him. 'Then she wasn't one,' he said. He could feel Mister D's sightless eyes on him, through the black glasses. He swallowed. 'I mean, to all intents and purposes she isn't a Rymer. She's never done any Rymer-type things.'

'She came here,' said Mister D.

'Nobody invited her,' said Thomas, hoping he was on the right track. 'She just stumbled in.'

'It doesn't matter,' said Mister D.

'Yes, it does,' said Thomas, more confidently, because he'd heard a tiny note of doubt in Mister D's voice. 'That very thing saved my life once, in Uncouther country. She can't be a Rymer. She doesn't fit.'

'Nevertheless, it's her name I have on my list,' said Mister D, crossly. 'Rymer or not . . .' He leaned towards Thomas, who felt a coldness creeping over his scalp, icing the blood in his veins. 'Don't you be playing games with Mister D, my child, or it might be the worse for you.'

'But surely Thomas is right. You can only take a declared Rymer, if a Rymer is what your files say,' chimed in Old Gal. 'Not one who hasn't even realised she's one yet, who hasn't been invited, who doesn't fit at all.'

'I have to take one,' said Mister D, coldly. 'It's on my job list. And she's the closest and most suitable one.'

'There is another Rymer here,' said Old Gal, bleakly. 'Here, in the Hidden World.'

'You mean James Grimm,' said Mister D. 'Poor-quality Rymer, that one.'

'But a Rymer, still.'

'That is so.'

'We won't let you take Alice, and you've said yourself you're not taking Thomas,' said Old Gal, defiantly. 'What choice have you got?'

There was a tiny silence. 'You forget who you're speaking to,' hissed Mister D.

'That I do not,' said Old Gal.

'You know what might happen.'

'Yes,' sighed Old Gal. Thomas's heart raced. What did Mister D mean? He glanced at the twins. They seemed as bewildered as he did.

'Very well. I will have to consult my files. This is all most irregular. I am not pleased.'

He was about to go when Thomas suddenly said, 'Sir, please – may I ask you a question?'

Mister D said, 'You may ask. I may not answer.'

'There is a ghost, sir – a most kind and gentle ghost on the island who goes by the name of Doctor Noname, because he is forgotten. I promised I would ask you, sir. I owe him a great debt, and I wondered if you might look in your files and see whether . . .'

'Foolish boy,' said Mister D, angrily, 'That is not possible. In any case, you already have the means to find out. He left something behind, something you have already seen. It will give you his name and his salvation. No, don't even think of asking me what, or I will lose my temper. You are a most importunate and insolent young man.'

And without another word, he turned on his heel and limped out of the cottage, followed by the robotic Riders. An instant later, they heard the car start up again, and when they rushed over to the window to take a look, they saw the procession moving slowly off, down the hill and towards the river, in the direction that Grimm and his accomplices had fled.

Patch gave a deep sigh. 'By the horns of Pan, that was a close one, Thomas! Fancy asking him that!'

'I had to,' said Thomas.

'But what did he mean?' said Pinch. 'What thing do we have of Doctor Noname? He didn't give anything to us, did he?'

'No,' said Thomas. 'Nothing at all, as far as I know.'

Old Gal had dropped to her knees beside a still-unconscious Alice, and felt her pulse and then her forehead. 'Hmm. She's getting warmer. That's good. I think she'll be all right, though I'll have to nurse her for a while yet.'

'Mother,' said Pinch, 'what did Mister D mean, when he asked you if you knew what might happen?'

Old Gal answered, impatiently, 'He meant just what he said.'

'But what—' began Thomas.

'It's time *you* went home,' she said. 'More than time. And I don't mean the Apple Tree Café, either. I mean London.'

'But I've got to find out about Doctor Noname . . .'

'We'll investigate,' said Old Gal, firmly. 'It will be a job for Pinch and Patch, something to keep their minds off things.' Her tone softened. 'You, my dear boy, have to go back to London. This very evening. Without delay.'

'But surely now—'

She gave a snort. 'If you're going on Mister D's word,' she said, 'it's a mistake. He was angry with you just now. If he doesn't get hold of Grimm, or if he decides he doesn't want to, and comes back and you're still here, in the Hidden World, he could take you.' She paused. 'That's what he meant by what might happen. It means he can change his mind. He can alter his files. It's not safe for you to be here, Thomas, not any more. Not for a while.'

At that moment, the door opened and Gareth rushed in, followed rather more sedately by Adverse Camber and Angelica Eyebright.

'Thank goodness you're OK,' Gareth kept repeating, as he hugged Thomas, over and over. 'Thank goodness.' Then he saw Alice. 'Oh, dear, poor child. Who is she? What's happened?'

Thomas explained, rapidly.

Gareth said, 'Poor little girl . . . what's going to happen to her now?'

'I'll nurse her back to health,' said Old Gal. 'And then she can go back to her own world, like Thomas.'

'But—' began Thomas.

'No arguments,' said Angelica, firmly.

'But Alice doesn't have any family left,' said Thomas. 'Patch said her parents were dead and her only relative is that awful Grimm person, and Mister D's gone after him now, and . . .'

'Don't concern yourself with it, Thomas,' said Angelica. 'We will make sure she's OK.'

'Mister D said she was a Rymer,' said Thomas. 'Is that true?'

'It might be,' said Angelica, glancing at Alice, whose colour was slowly returning, though her eyes stayed shut.

'Some people – it takes time with them,' said Adverse.

'Then maybe she can stay in the Hidden World and learn about it,' said Thomas, trying to speak calmly, though his stomach heaved with a sudden, sharp jealousy.

Old Gal smiled. 'She's not ready for that,' she said, gently.

'Definitely not,' said Angelica. 'Later, maybe.'

'Much later,' chimed in Adverse.

'You will be here again before she's ready,' said Angelica, gravely. 'And that's the truth, Thomas.'

He looked at her and at the others, and knew suddenly that it was, actually, the truth. He looked down at Alice and suddenly felt ashamed of his earlier jealousy. He said, 'Dad, maybe . . . I thought . . . maybe Alice could come and stay with us for a while? I mean, when she's better?'

Gareth blinked. 'Well, yes, why not? Why not, indeed? Yes, a splendid idea.'

He sounded surprised, thought Thomas, but then so am I. Why on earth did I say that? I hadn't planned on saying it at all!

'That's a very good idea,' said Angelica,

looking relieved. 'A very good one. Now, Thomas, I'm afraid we're going to have to go. Just a quick goodbye to everyone in the village, and then we're off.'

'Please,' burst in Patch, 'please, can't Pinch and I come with you, to see Thomas off? Please?'

Angelica glanced at Old Gal, who nodded. 'Only to the border, then,' she said. 'And no further. And I mean that, children, do you hear?'

FIFTEEN

It was a sad little party that jolted along the road in Metallicus, some time later. Thomas and the twins sat huddled close to each other in the back, too miserable to talk, while Adverse and Gareth were in the front. Though they'd started off trying to jolly the children along, they'd given up by now.

The goodbyes in the village had been very sad. Everyone was sorry to see Thomas and his father go. They'd been showered with presents – cakes and books, and a fat package Thomas had been told not to open till he got home. But for Thomas, all of it happened in a blur. He'd miss Owlchurch, and the people, and the shops, and the river, and all the adventures he'd had, and oh, everything! But the thing he would miss most of all, never mind magic or adventures or anything else, was his friendship with Pinch and Patch. He thought about what Pinch had said, about Mum's song and what it had meant to him, about always being friends. And he wished with all his heart, with every bit of himself, that somehow things might change, that a miracle might happen, and that somehow he would not have to say goodbye to Pinch and Patch at the border, but be with them, friends for always.

As they crested a rise, Thomas looked back and saw, to one side of the river, Owlchurch, nestled cosily in its fold of hill; and sparkling over the other side of the river, Aspire, with its elegant towers and spires. He'd even miss Aspire, he thought, and its smart, rather chilly mayors, Mr Tamblin and the Lady Pandora, who'd helped him out a couple of times.

He blinked. For there, gliding along the road towards them, was a motorbike. Not the sinister ones the Riders rode, but the elegant, neat little thing owned by the Lady Pandora. She was riding it, and behind her, smiling, a paper package under his arm, was Mr Tamblin.

Adverse stopped the car and wound down the window. Lady Pandora and Mr Tamblin hopped off the bike and came to the window.

'Well, well,' Mr Tamblin said in his silky voice, peering in, 'quite a party we have here, eh!'

'Just give it to him, Tamblin,' snapped the Lady Pandora. She looked a little hot and bothered – the most bothered Thomas had ever seen her. 'We're in a hurry.'

'Astrolir and Fustian have just been spotted trying to sneak back in,' said Tamblin, nonchalantly. 'No sign of that other fellow. He's still running from Mister D, I'd guess. But there's word that there's a bit of trouble looming with some renegades from all over the place, thinking they can invade. Got to nip that in the bud, all of us, what?' He handed the package to Adverse. 'This is for the kids,' he added.

'We found it hiding in Dr Fantasos's workshop,' said Lady Pandora. 'It got in through a crack in the floor. Hinkypunk told us you might need it.' She smiled at Thomas. 'So you're leaving us, True Tom? A pity, but there it is. Still, we enjoyed meeting you. Do come again.'

'Thank you,' murmured Thomas, smiling despite himself at her casual tone.

'Yes, do,' said Tamblin. 'Toodle-oo, chaps!' They returned to their bike and took off in a scatter of pebbles, Mr Tamblin's white silk muffler waving in the breeze, Lady Pandora's long black hair streaming out behind her.

'Those ones,' growled Adverse, 'never know when they're serious or not,' and he handed the package over to Thomas. 'Take care when you open it, never know with them,' he added.

Thomas unwrapped the package. He gave a little gasp. For there, lying in the folds of paper, was the lost book!

'What's that?' said Gareth, from the front.

'It's a book about the Ghost World, Dad,' said Thomas. 'We used it to ask questions before, but it escaped.' He opened the book. 'Watch this. Please, book,' he went on, 'please tell us how to help a homeless soul, wandering the worlds, so that he may go back to his own place.'

The book stayed blank. Thomas asked again. Still the pages stayed blank. Once more, he asked . . . then suddenly, on to the paper came some words, so faintly that Thomas could only just read them. *It is a most fine day, Rymer. But I cannot answer. My maker's spirit is weak now. I cannot* . . . Then the words petered out.

'Please, book, please,' said Patch. 'Please try, try again.'

But Thomas was thinking hard. He said, 'Those words – I've heard them before.'

'What do you mean?' said Pinch.

'It is a most fine day, Rymer,' repeated Thomas.

'Of course,' said Patch. 'The book said that to you before.'

'Yes, but somewhere else . . .' said Thomas. 'And I know where, too,' he went on, as light broke in on him at last. 'On the Island of Ghosts. I heard Doctor Noname say it!'

'You don't mean . . .' said Pinch, slowly. 'You don't mean what I think you mean?'

'Yes! Doctor Noname wrote this book!' said Thomas, excitedly. 'I'm sure of it!' He closed the book and looked at the front. 'That's what Mister D meant! This is the thing that belonged to Doctor Noname! In fact, I think Doctor Noname was the wily wizard of maximum repute who wrote this book!'

'Well, what's his real name, then?' said Patch.

Thomas looked – front, back, flipping the pages. Nothing. There was no clue at all. 'Oh dear, and I was so sure . . .' he said, glumly.

There was a little cough. Gareth said, gently, 'If I might make a suggestion – some people like to write under pen-names: they don't like to use their real name on their books.'

'But Dad, there's no pen-name, just the wily wizard thing,' said Thomas.

'I meant to say that sometimes people make up a code which, if you know it, can reveal their actual name. Now that *wily wizard of maximum repute* title sounds dodgy to me – I mean, either it's a most conceited boast, or it's meant to hide something, it's a kind of joke . . . What I mean is,' he went on, seeing the children's bewildered faces, 'is that his name is somewhere in that phrase. Do you see? I mean, perhaps his first name is William, or something – he's used wily, to cover that.'

Everyone stared at him. Then Adverse laughed. 'I do believe you're on to something there, Gareth,' he said.

'Yes! Yes!' said Thomas. 'Oh Dad, I bet that's it! I bet his name's something like that!'

'There could be any kinds of combinations, though,' said Gareth, apologetically. 'It's like doing a cryptic crossword or something. It can send you crazy.'

But the children didn't listen. They were too busy trying out all sorts of combinations. So busy were they that they forgot about being miserable, forgot about the time passing, or that the countryside outside was changing, that somehow the air was starting to feel different, the Hidden World beginning slowly, almost invisibly, to lose its outline, its colours, it shapes . . .

So Thomas had a big shock when finally Metallicus stopped, abruptly. He raised his head and saw that there was a kind of glassy mist in front of them, and that through this mist, as if deep in a tarnished mirror, he could see a street he knew, a house he hadn't thought about in a long time. His heart raced. He said, 'Please – do we really have to go? Please, can't we stay?'

'No,' said Adverse, sternly, and the single word made Thomas realise, as none other had, that there was no hope and there would be no miracle. 'We will leave you both here,' said Adverse, 'but we will see you again, Thomas Trew, our own dear Rymer, and that is a promise.'

'Yes,' said Thomas, sadly, as they all climbed out of Metallicus. He was still holding the book. And it was in that moment, when all hope had fled from him, that it came to him. He was sure what the ghost's name was, now, though he wasn't sure how he knew.

He opened the book. 'Did Max Williams write this book? Dr Maximilian Williams, a great wizard?'

There was a breathless pause; and then, suddenly the book erupted with words, tumbling over each other. *Yes! I am the book of Dr Maximilian Williams, that is the name of my maker, and because you have found his name, his spirit may return through me.*

'How?' breathed Thomas.

It is simple, scrawled the book. *All you need say,*

is, Max Williams, go in peace, your home awaits you, you have fulfilled your afterlife's task. If one has the name, said the book, *so much more is simple. So much, because then there is no forgetting, and the memory holds the immortal spirit fast, and bright. Hurry, boy, hurry, for soon it will be past the point of no return.*

So Thomas said the words; and as he did so, it seemed to them all that quite suddenly, through the pages of the book flashed a picture, at first blurry but soon getting clearer and clearer, of a tall old man in black robes and a black velvet cap, his hands outstretched towards them. As the picture got clearer, they saw that the mask that had covered half his face had disappeared, and they could see his features clearly. Doctor Noname – Dr Max Williams – had a nice face, with bright, smiling eyes and a high, creased forehead.

On the book's pages appeared some words. *You have freed me, Thomas Trew. You have freed me from the forgetting; you have given me a bridge home.*

'I owe you my life,' said Thomas, simply.

'I could not bear to think of you homeless and lost.'

You are a great Rymer, said the book. *Perhaps the greatest Rymer who ever lived. You will never be forgotten, Thomas Trew, and nor will your friends. Goodbye, my dears, goodbye . . .*

'Goodbye,' the children chorused, as slowly the words faded, the picture vanished. But as Thomas closed the book, suddenly, on the front cover, before *a wily wizard of maximum repute,* appeared some new words, in letters of gold: *Dr Maximilian Williams.* And these letters did not fade, but stayed bright and clear and glowing.

Thomas gave a little sigh. He said, 'I think you'd better take the book back to Monotype's bookshop. It belongs here, in this world.' He paused. 'Everyone should know about it. Everyone should remember Dr Max Williams, so he will never be forgotten again.'

'He won't be, I promise you that,' said Adverse Camber, gravely. 'The book and his memory will be held in very high honour indeed.'

Thomas nodded. 'Thank you.' He turned to Pinch and Patch. 'Goodbye,' he said, trying not to let his voice break. 'I hope we see each other again, very soon.'

Pinch and Patch nodded, too miserable to speak.

'I guess we'd better go, Dad,' said Thomas. He had to face the world out there. It wasn't a world he wanted to face, without his friends or his mother. But he wouldn't be quite alone. There was Dad. And there might be Alice, later. Even Lily. And one day, he'd return here. There was nothing surer than that.

So he took his father's hand and, quietly, the two of them walked towards the London street they could see gloaming through the glassy mist. But just as they reached it, Thomas turned around for one last look, at Pinch and Patch and Adverse, standing beside Metallicus.

'See you soon,' he said. 'See you very soon,'

he repeated, as if it was a spell that must come true, and he saw the hope light up briefly in their eyes. Metallicus hooted, once, mournfully, as if it too was saying goodbye, then Thomas and his father walked through the mist into the London street.

And when he turned around again, the Hidden World had vanished, as completely as though it had never been there at all.

SIXTEEN

Time passed. Days, weeks. Thomas went back to school. It wasn't much fun. He didn't feel like talking to anyone, and he couldn't concentrate on anything. He spent a lot of time sitting at his desk staring out of the window, dreaming about Pinch and Patch and the Hidden World, and wishing he could be back there.

At home, things had changed. Gareth's experience in the Hidden World made him more confident in the Obvious World, and he decided to open his own café. Lily came to visit them often. She was going to run the café with Gareth. They had already rented an old shop and were doing it up. Thomas knew now that

Lily and his dad would probably end up being together, and he didn't mind much any more. Lily wasn't that bad, once you got to know her, though she'd never be like Mum.

Just as she'd promised, he'd seen Mum in his dreams a couple of times, and that had helped, a bit. But just a bit.

There was no word from the Hidden World at all. Nothing, not even about Alice. Thomas did not know what had happened to her. It might be Alice learning about the Hidden World now, Alice having adventures, Alice playing with Pinch and Patch ... Thomas tried to stop himself from thinking these things, but it was hard. He knew his dad and Lily were worried about him. They tried to get him to make new friends. But he didn't feel like it. He didn't feel like much, really. It was as though nothing was quite real, as though he was in a slow, dull dream. He wished with all his heart that he could wake from it and be in his bedroom above the Apple Tree Café, ready for another adventure with Pinch and Patch.

After school and on the weekends, he sat in his room and looked endlessly at the books the Hidden Worlders had given him as presents. They were big books, with lots of illustrations, and really beautiful. There was a book about each of the different kinds of people who lived in the Hidden World, and about their countries. The books didn't behave like Hidden World books any more. They didn't speak and the pictures didn't come to life. But the illustrations were really detailed, and there was a smell about the books that reminded him really strongly of the world they'd come from.

They had given him another present. It too was a book. A fat leather-bound book, which had on it, in gold, *Thomas Trew the Rymer – His Book*. But there was nothing on any of the pages. They were all blank.

'I suppose it's to write in,' Gareth said. 'A kind of diary, maybe? Perhaps that's a good idea? It might take your mind off things.'

'No way,' shouted Thomas. 'I don't want my mind taken off things! And there's nothing to write about, anyway! Not now!'

And then, one rainy Saturday morning, everything changed. As usual, Thomas was sitting in his room leafing through the books, when his father came in. He had a strange look on his face.

'Just got a phone call, Thomas. From the local hospital. They say they've got a young girl there who's asking for us. It's Alice Grimm! She was dropped off there early this morning. The hospital say they don't know who left her. They say she's rather weak, but otherwise well, and that she'll be able to leave in a day or two. Is it still OK with you, if she comes here?'

Thomas shrugged. 'I suppose so.'

'You don't sound very keen . . .'

'It's OK, Dad, I don't mind.'

'But . . .' Gareth began, then thought better

of it. 'OK. Do you want to come with me to the hospital to see her?'

'Can I go another time?' said Thomas. 'I feel a bit tired, today.' It wasn't true, and he felt bad about it, but he wasn't really ready for this. Not yet.

Gareth sighed. 'OK. That's fine. I'll go with Lily.' He hesitated, but Thomas had picked up a book and was pretending to read it.

'Right, I'll see you later, then,' he said, reluctantly. 'An hour or two at the most.'

'Fine,' said Thomas, not looking up from his book. But when his father left the house – he heard the front door slam – he got up again and went to the window. He saw his father getting into the car and driving away, and suddenly he wished he'd gone with him. He could talk to Alice about Owlchurch. About Pinch and Patch. About everything. He was an idiot to be jealous. An idiot.

Across the street, a little yellow car pulled in at the kerb. It was a battered, old-fashioned thing, painted all over with bright designs, and it pulled a kind of home-made trailer, which was filled with boxes. Thomas watched it idly. He'd never seen the car before. And the house where it had stopped had been empty for quite some time. Perhaps these people were moving in?

In the next instant, he let out a yell. For the car front door opened and someone stepped out. Someone very familiar! He raced out of his room, down the stairs, out of the house and into the street below, not caring that he was in his slippers or that it was raining, or anything.

'Old Gal! Is that really you? Oh, what are you doing here? You look different – your clothes . . .' That was true. She was much neater than he'd ever seen her, though still rather shabby, her tall, thin form wrapped in a raincoat and trousers, her hair sort of brushed. 'What are you . . .?'

Then he stopped, his eyes round, a hand to his mouth, for Pinch and Patch had come tumbling out of the back of the car. They didn't look very different, though their hair had been slicked down a bit. For a moment, he couldn't speak; then he rushed at them, and the three of them hugged and shouted and laughed, while Old Gal stood watching them with an amused expression on her face.

'Are you here for a visit?' Thomas said, when at last the noise had stopped.

Pinch shook his head, solemnly, though his eyes twinkled. Patch said, 'No.'

'Oh. Did you come because of Alice?' said Thomas, crestfallen.

'No, no,' said Pinch.

'To deliver something, then?'

'Thomas,' said Patch, crossly, 'be quiet or we'll never be able to tell you!' She looked at him, her eyes shining like stars. 'Thomas – we've come to live here!'

For a moment, Thomas thought he'd heard wrong. He stared at the twins. 'What do you mean?'

'We've come to live here,' said Pinch, impatiently. He jerked a thumb at the house behind him. 'In this house.'

'We're going to live just across the road from you, Thomas,' said Patch, excitedly.

Thomas stared at them, then at Old Gal. 'But I thought . . . I thought . . .' he said, weakly.

'You thought we weren't allowed to live in the Obvious World,' said Old Gal, calmly. 'Normally, that's true. But as you know, I was awarded the Horns of Pan. One of the things it means is that you can live in both worlds, if you want to.' She paused. 'I can't say living in the Obvious World has ever really appealed to me. But I couldn't stand to see the miserable faces of these two a day longer. And I thought, well, until you can go back to our world, we can come and live here. I talked to the others in Owlchurch, and they agreed. I'll open a business. And I may be able to collect a few unusual herbs and catch up with a few good wizards and witches, and learn a thing or two here, so it won't altogether be wasted time . . .'

'Oh, Mother,' said Patch, hugging her, 'you did it because you're just the nicest mother ever!'

'Yes,' said Pinch, 'you're fantastic!'

'You're really, really kind,' said Thomas, sincerely.

'Stuff and nonsense,' said Old Gal, sharply. 'Now you children stop gawping at each other like china dogs and help me carry our things inside, or we'll never get settled.'

'Yes, Mother,' shouted the twins, happily, and 'Yes, Mrs Gull,' sang out Thomas. And as they started unpacking the car together and carrying the luggage into the house, all the time talking nineteen to the dozen, Thomas thought that he had never felt happier in his whole life. He felt full to bursting with happiness, in fact. It seemed to drench everything around him in light, so that he hardly even noticed the rain still falling and the slippery pavement.

Suddenly, that grey, ordinary, rainy London street was the most beautiful thing he'd seen, and that ordinary, grey London house they were walking into, the best place he'd ever been. And as he talked with his best friends, Pinch and Patch, about the wonderful time they were going to have, a picture popped into his mind. It was of Adverse Camber and Angelica Eyebright, standing in his hall all those months ago. Yes, he thought. Someday, he was going to write that story. He was going to pick up that book with blank pages and he was going to write about his adventures in the Hidden World, and everything that had happened there, and of course all the people he'd met.

He knew now what the gift was that the Hidden World had given him, their newest Rymer. They had given him the gift of friendship and happiness. He knew now what kind of Rymer he was, too. For he he was going to give them something back; a wonderful, wonderful story, something that let everyone in the Hidden World know how much he loved being there. And that made everyone in the Obvious World realise what an amazing, magical and exciting world lay just beyond the borders of the everyday.

'Something wrong?' said Patch, a little anxiously, for Thomas stood stock-still with a box in his hands, looking into the distance.

'Nothing at all,' said Thomas, happily, snapping back to the glorious present.

'Well, there's something wrong with me,' groused Pinch. 'These are heavy boxes – and I'm hungry!'

'There's a baker just down the street,' said Thomas, laughing. 'And I've got a bit of money in my wallet. We could go and get a cake, or a pie or something.'

'Oh yes!' said Pinch. 'Yes, yes! I really want to try Obbo cakes – please, Mother, please . . .'

'Yes, yes, off you go,' said Old Gal, flapping at them. 'You hold things up more than help, anyway,' she called after them, as they ran off down the street, whooping and yelling with delight. 'Kids!' Old Gal muttered smiling broadly, and turned back to her unpacking.

Doors and windows were opening up and down the street. Everyone wanted to see what the commotion was. A few people frowned and told each other that a very noisy lot had moved into their quiet street. But others smiled and said how nice it was to see children enjoying themselves, even on a rainy day like this. But Thomas, Pinch and Patch didn't care one hoot for what anyone might say as they raced along, best friends together again, and all the unhappiness of the last few weeks was left far behind them.